Beneath Montana's Sky

DEBRA HOLLAND

Acknowledgments

As always, I have a fantastic team of people who support me and make my life better—far too many to mention here. Just know you are in my heart.
My special thanks and appreciation go to:

My Editors:
Louella Nelson
Linda Carroll-Bradd
Adela Brito

My Formatter:
Amy Atwell

My Family:
Honey Holland (my mom)
Hedy Codner (my aunt)
Larry Codner (my uncle)
for their sharp-eyed editing
and
Mindy Codner Freed (my cousin)
for making my life run more smoothly
and
Tim Holland (my brother)
for heroically stepping in to rescue me on deadline day

To the fans at Pioneer Hearts, a Facebook Historical Western Romance Author and Reader Site:
for their encouragement and fact finding.

and
Noah Michael Levine, for inspiration

FOUR YEARS BEFORE
THE MAIL-ORDER BRIDES OF THE WEST STORIES

AND

ELEVEN YEARS BEFORE
WILD MONTANA SKY
TAKES PLACE

<h1 style="text-align:center">Chapter One</h1>

⁂

SWEETWATER SPRINGS
MONTANA TERRITORY
October, 1882

John Carter stood in the cemetery in front of the three graves holding the caskets of the Sanders' family—his foreman and best friend, Andrew, his wife Dora, and their young daughter Marcy. Beside John, thirteen-year-old Nick Sanders only stared at the ground.

With his face ghost white, so the freckles on his nose stood out, and his blue-green eyes blank—the boy seemed almost too shocked and grief-stricken to comprehend what had happened two days earlier. Nick had remained on the ranch, instead of traveling to town with his family and thus avoided the fatal accident.

John knew all too well about the numbness that came after the initial spiking pain of sudden death. He flicked a glance at Marcy's small coffin, then just as quickly looked away, unable to bear the sight. His sister's coffin had been the same size. Old anguish and guilt twisted with fresh pain, and he thought the agony of his feelings might bring him to his knees.

He stiffened, needing to be strong, not only for his godson, orphaned now, but also for the rest of the close-knit community

1

of Sweetwater Springs—many of whom gathered around the graves. As the owner of the largest ranch and the descendent of one of the earliest families to settle in these parts, John was considered a town leader.

A cold breeze blew, bringing the earthy smell of fresh-turned dirt, flapping the black skirts of the teary-eyed women, and ruffling the hair of the men who stood with their heads bowed, their hats held in front of their chests.

The sadness emanating from the mourners was so strong, seeming to hover like storm clouds in the milky-gray sky, thick and heavy and swollen as if with anguished tears. Even Reverend Norton, standing at the head of the three graves, a prayer book in his bare hands, wasn't unmoved. As the minister recited the burial service, his voice quavered in several places before he took an audible breath to continue.

Nick shuddered, a visible shaking of his wiry body.

John dropped a comforting hand on the boy's shoulder, so very grateful Nick hadn't gone with his family on that fateful wagon trip to town. For the hundredth time since he'd heard the news, John asked himself, *What could have happened to cause the accident? Did something spook the horses—a panther or a bear? Had something happened to Andrew himself? Did the man suddenly take sick?* The road in that spot had been a heavily-forested steep grade, slick with ice. But if Andrew had driven carefully, as John knew without a doubt his friend had, there wasn't a reason he could see for the cause of the accident. He wondered if they'd ever know the truth.

I should have persuaded them to stay home for a few more days.

But after an initial cold spell, they'd experienced a few weeks of Indian summer, and before being cooped up for the long winter, Dora had wanted to head into town, visit with Mary Norton, the minister's wife, and go to the mercantile for some shopping. Andrew hadn't been a man to deny his pretty wife anything. And why should he? The snow had melted, the skies looked clear, the sun was warm for an autumn day.

Reverend Norton, the black frock coat his parishioners had given him the previous Christmas flapping in the wind, closed his prayer book, bringing John back to the pain of the present. The minister's austere bearded face, made even more harsh with sorrow, belied his gentle tone. "With love in our hearts, we bid a final farewell to Andrew, Dora, and Marcy, knowing they are safe in heaven. We who are left behind will deeply mourn them. May the Lord give us strength and comfort to carry on." With a nod and a compassionate glance around at his congregation, lingering on Nick, the minister brought the service to a close.

At her husband's side, Mary Norton dabbed her eyes with a handkerchief. In her other hand, she carried a small bunch of bright autumn leaves, their edges flat from being pressed between the pages of a book. The orange, gold, and burgundy colors contrasted with the browns and grays of the season. She and Dora Sanders, who'd been the schoolteacher before her marriage, had a close friendship, and John figured Mrs. Norton's pain might be great, indeed.

But the minister's wife didn't see Dora every day like I saw Andrew. The two ladies hadn't grown up together.... John remembered he and Andrew as boys—hunting, fishing, riding, roping, and getting into trouble.

John was no stranger to death, even sudden death. The small burial ground at the ranch held his grandparents, parents, and sister. He, like Nick, was alone. More than anyone, he knew what it was like to stand bereft at an open grave—the last of your family.

A woman sobbed loudly.

Mrs. Norton tucked her handkerchief inside her sleeve and separated the leaves into three small clumps. They quivered in her hands before she tossed each bunch into the graves, where they fluttered down to rest atop the plain wooden caskets.

Under his hand, John felt Nick's body shake, but the boy didn't make a sound.

John had to repress a similar shudder before guiding Nick

away from the graves. Neither needed to see the dirt tossed over the coffins.

As they moved through the crowd, he tipped his hat and muttered "thank you" to the fleeting touches on his or Nick's arms…the stammered expressions of condolence.

His cook, Edgar McKnight, had scrounged up a repast for any who might undertake the long drive out to the ranch. But John doubted many would attend. Not that they wouldn't want to, but with the accident fresh in their minds and the threat of a coming storm in the air, most would wisely choose to remain safe at home.

Better it just be him and Nick and his cowhands—the ones who'd miss Andrew, Dora, and Marcy every day for a long time to come.

The scrape of shovels and the thumping of dirt pouring on the coffins made Nick glance behind him, his expression bleak.

John's stomach ached as if someone had punched a stone inside him and left it there.

The boy's my responsibility now.

John had to stand in place of father and mother, a task for which he was woefully inadequate. *What the heck am I going to do?*

At age thirty-two, he had no training as a parent. The responsibility of raising the boy pressed down on him as the sky did the land, and John felt alone.

Chapter Two

SWEETWATER SPRINGS
April, 1883

After a long day of branding the January-born calves, John rode with a group of his cowboys toward the barn, fighting exhaustion and low spirits. Both arms ached from reining the horse and throwing the lasso and his legs from continually urging the gelding after the skittish animals. He'd missed far too many heelers today, having to make second and third attempts to catch the calves' hind legs. Andrew would have ribbed him mercilessly.

But his friend's absence was the reason for John's lack of concentration, and he wasn't the only one. His cowboys were just as rattled. Branding all the young animals and castrating the bull calves had taken twice as long as usual.

Dusk was settling. A solitary cloud turned golden in the purple sky, looking as lonely as he felt right now, even though he rode with men as familiar to him as his battered Stetson. A sharp wind whistled around the group, ruffling the dried grass to show the green shoots underneath. Clumps of snow lingered in the shade of the trees. He tilted his head into the wind to avoid having his hat blow off.

Calves were the lifeblood of the ranch, and from the births

the last three months, the ranch was going to have a good season—although plenty could go wrong between now and shipping off the cattle to market on the train. For the first time, the cowhands wouldn't have to undertake a long cattle drive. The new railroad had changed everything, making life in Montana Territory far easier. He and Andrew had talked of how different the coming year would be with not having to spend the weeks away from the ranch.

With the extra time at home, they'd planned to plant several acres of alfalfa and hay—becoming farmers as well as ranchers. But his friend wouldn't be here to see the changes. The absence of Andrew's steady presence at his side not only reminded John of his personal loss but also robbed him of the satisfaction he'd always felt in past years at branding time.

Thinking of Andrew, John glanced over at Nick. The boy rode Skinner, his chestnut gelding. Like John, his head was dipped into the wind. But unlike John, he kept his eyes downcast.

The boy had done the work of a man today. Couldn't complain about that. Nick had roped better than John, showing a single-minded determination and not even cracking a smile at the comical moments.

Nick had always been on the silent side, although a deep thinker, prone to asking curious or probing questions. But his family's death had rendered him practically mute. He only volunteered information when necessary, which seemed about once a week. When asked a direct question, he answered with as few words as possible. John had more than a few cowboys like that, but Nick's reticence was an unsettling change in the boy, who'd retreated like a prairie dog into his hole.

John had felt helpless to comfort the boy after the loss of his family. In the months since the deaths, he'd done everything he could think of to console his godson, to help the boy cope. He didn't know how to reach Nick, let alone assuage his own grief.

Sometimes, he found his steps turning to the foreman's little house before he remembered his best friend wasn't there.

Everyone missed Dora's friendly smile and the treats she'd bake for them. She'd provided a feminine presence for their gang of cowboys, who'd all respected and maybe had a bit of a crush on the feisty woman. That and her cookies and pies…not things his practical cook tended to indulge in.

And everyone had adored Marcy. His throat tightened remembering her gapped-tooth grin and the rag doll she dragged with her everywhere. Without the presence of womenfolk, the ranch was missing a heart.

John sent another concerned glance at Nick, riding slumped in the saddle next to him. "You worked hard today, Nick."

The boy nodded, his expression unchanging.

John sucked in a breath before venturing on. "Your father would have been proud." He hadn't spoken for Andrew before now. Wasn't sure how Nick would take it.

This time, the boy's nod was shorter. He looked down and wouldn't meet John's eyes. His Adam's apple moved as if he swallowed an emotion.

Did I say the right thing? With Nick, John felt he was fording a stream, hopping from one slippery rock to another, apt to slip off into the water that was deeper than he realized.

John pondered the question that had been on his mind ever since the boy had come into his care. *How do I help him?*

The obvious solution—work too hard to think. God knew they labored hard every day. They'd all thrown themselves into their work, trying to dull the pain. But that remedy wasn't enough; the boy was lost to them.

He chewed on a new solution Mrs. Norton had hinted to him two Sundays ago. *A wife.*

Her suggestion had settled in his mind—an idea to mull over on long rides or before he fell asleep at night. Surely, a mother figure for Nick would help the boy. Having a woman around again would do all the men good, including him.

And a wife would be even more of a blessing. Someone to soothe everyone's grief, take charge of his neglected home, provide him some companionship, and warm his bed. The thought caused his body to heat. *Give me children.*

Not for the first time, John listed his requirements for a bride: kindness and compassion, the ability to adapt to the hard life of the ranch, attractive, a good companion, and most importantly, a woman who'd love him and whom he could love.

While John instinctively believed the idea of a wife was a good one, the execution of a courtship wasn't possible.

There's no such woman in Sweetwater Springs.

In fact, there were no available women in the area, unless you counted Widow Mattis with her seven children and seven teeth in her mouth, or the three fourteen-year-olds, all of whom he'd have to wait on until they grew up to a marriageable age. And he wouldn't be the only man in the area with his eye on those girls. He'd be thirty-five by the time they were seventeen, a huge difference in age. And he'd have plenty of competition. Probably fifty men in the vicinity of Sweetwater Springs wished for a wife.

Three years would be too late. Nick needed a mother figure now.

I need to go East.

Sixty-something years ago, John's grandparents had traveled months to reach Montana Territory in a covered wagon. But with the train newly come to the area, John could make the journey back to Boston in a matter of days. Over the years, he'd conducted a sporadic correspondence with his grandmother's youngest sister, his Great-Aunt Hester, who'd issued many invitations to visit.

A big city holds a multitude of women.

He debated whether or not to take Nick with him. But the boy had experienced enough changes lately, and John was going courtin', which was no place for his godson. Hopefully it wouldn't take him long to find a bride who'd fit his requirements, woo her, and bring her home to the ranch. After all, he wasn't demanding great beauty and wealth.

Great-Aunt Hester can evaluate candidates and single out potential brides. Just like going to a stock auction, 'cept maybe the process will take me a few weeks longer. I'll leave at the end of April when the branding's done.

Chapter Three

BOSTON
April, 1883

Twenty-one-year old Pamela Burke-Smythe approached the ballroom of the Sofit mansion, lent to The Society for Widows and Orphans, searching for her best friend, Elizabeth Hamilton. If the choice had been hers, she would have stayed at home, happily reading. But this evening—in support of the society— was the culmination of many weeks of effort by her and Elizabeth, as well as other members of the organization. She needed to be here tonight, if only to ensure everything went as they'd planned.

For the first hour, Pamela had resolved to avoid conversation and dancing by seeing to the various tasks involved in organizing a charity ball. In reality, the other women could have done some of the last-minute details just as well, but she knew they'd rather greet the arrivals, socialize, and anticipate partners for the dancing. She saw her friend in a group of ladies and walked over to them, exchanging greetings.

Elizabeth pulled her aside. "No one has quite your touch with entertaining, setting a lovely table, and anticipating guests' pleasure." She reached up and tucked a wayward tendril of Pamela's brown hair behind her ear. "Your skills have done much to benefit this evening. But I insist that you do not hide yourself away tonight like you usually do."

Pamela didn't answer. Her friend knew her too well.

A flurry of arrivals drew Elizabeth's attention to the doorway. "I must go. I shall save you a chair by mine, dear Pam. Come as soon as you're satisfied that everything is ready."

"I will." *I'm sure I can find plenty to do first.* She nodded and waved the other ladies off to their diversions.

For a moment, Pamela watched her friend. Although she was one of several hostesses who were greeting the guests, Elizabeth drew all eyes with her blonde beauty, sparkling blue eyes, and gracious manners.

Feeling plain and dumpy, even in an off-white silk gown in almost the latest style, Pamela sighed and turned away to double check on tasks that didn't really need doing. She crossed the vast ballroom to see if the musicians had the correct order of music and that none of the flower arrangements—hothouse roses, ferns, and baby's breath—drooped. She descended to the kitchen, walking up and down the long tables to make sure the trays of delectable food were laid out to appeal to the eyes as well as the palate. She oversaw the first of the waiters bringing out trays of champagne glasses. Forty minutes later, she was gratified to know everything was ready for the guests, and the festivities proceeded like clockwork.

Once she'd run out of things to inspect and out of excuses as well, Pamela reluctantly headed back into the ballroom, as a participant this time. She paused in the doorway, hearing the strains of a Strauss waltz. By the light of the three dazzling crystal chandeliers and the sconces on the walls, couples circled the dance floor in each other's arms, while others stood or sat in the gold Versailles chairs along the edges of the room, talking and sipping champagne.

With satisfaction, Pamela surveyed the packed space. She could barely see the terrazzo floor. The turnout for the charity ball meant more funds to help widows and orphans, which made all the weeks of work worth the effort. With slow steps, she moved along the wall, nodding at people she knew, and searching through the crowd for Elizabeth.

She found her friend on the dance floor, swept in circles by Gregory Markham, who was considered the best dancer of their set of friends, able to move his partner about the floor in a firm but respectful hold, and skillfully turn her at a fast speed that just bordered on shocking their elders. But since he deftly avoided other couples, no one ever complained.

Pamela slid through a trio of elderly gentlemen until she was close to the couple. The gaslight gleamed over Elizabeth's golden hair and sparkled on the diamonds around her neck and on her ears and wrists. Tonight was the first time her twenty-year-old friend had worn the Hamilton diamonds since her mother passed away two years ago during the influenza epidemic that had also claimed Elizabeth's father and fiancé. Her gown of ice blue satin and peach lace enhanced the blue of her eyes, and the exercise flushed her cheeks a becoming shade of pink.

Elizabeth laughed and chatted with Gregory, free of the constraint she'd have with most other men. Gregory was no longer a potential suitor, for he'd recently become engaged to their friend Sylvia Jordan.

Although she wouldn't mind dancing with Gregory, Pamela didn't like balls. She disliked the press of people, the watchful stares of the matrons who were quick to pounce on any behavior of which they disapproved, and the effort to make conversation with eligible men. Most of all, she hated being a wallflower except for when one of her brothers' friends would ask her to dance, or one of Elizabeth's rejected suitors solicited her hand because she was the nearest woman in the vicinity after her friend was led onto the dance floor by a triumphant swain.

Even worse was when two men approached Elizabeth, obviously scheming to dance with her. But since she often turned down male requests to remain talking with Pamela, her suitors had learned a good strategy was for them to ask both ladies, and after the dance was over, to switch partners, so each had a chance with the beautiful heiress.

"Pamela." Roly-poly, Henry Felton, a friend of her brother's, planted himself in front of her, forcing her away from her ruminations. "Mother is insisting I dance tonight."

The expression on his round face was so miserable that Pamela couldn't help but laugh. "Your mother has decided it's time for you to marry, Henry. She told us so at the last society tea."

"Take pity on me, Pamela," he begged, addressing her with the familiarity of friends who'd known each other from the time they'd sported gaps in their front teeth.

She suppressed an inner sigh. Dancing with Henry, who had two left feet, could be a trying and sometimes embarrassing ordeal.

"Please?" He made puppy dog eyes at her, but since the orbs in question were green and protruding, he looked more like a frog.

The thought made her hold in a chuckle.

The next dance started, a Strauss quadrille. Not able to actually say *yes* to his invitation because she felt the *no* so strongly, Pamela just held out a gloved hand and forced a weak smile.

He gave a jerky bow and led them to their places. For the first slow measures, Henry was almost able to stay on the beat, and Pamela began to relax.

Then the tempo changed. In the next move, Henry stepped on her toes.

Pamela winced. She pulled him to the right before they collided with an elderly couple. He steered her in the wrong direction twice, trod on her other foot, and spun her entirely too fast one time, and too slow several others. The floor around them cleared as couples headed for safer ground.

Her cheeks heated at the spectacle they must be making, and Pamela prayed for the music to end. With the close of the final measure, she couldn't rush off the dance floor fast enough. At the edge, she turned to give Henry a polite goodbye smile.

With a grateful glance, Henry thanked her, pulling out his handkerchief to wipe the perspiration off his face. "Mother was watching us."

During an awkward turn, Pamela had seen Mrs. Felton wince and shake her head, a pained expression on her face. "You should go talk to your mother. Tell her you're going to seek out ladies and *converse* instead of dance. Perhaps now, she'll be more receptive of the idea."

"Excellent plan. Excellent." He rubbed his hands together. "She's bound to have witnessed the debacle I almost made, probably would have if you hadn't pointed me in the right direction a time or two."

More than a time or two. But she didn't say so. Henry was a good-natured sort, and she'd practically known him her whole life, so she couldn't be annoyed with him. But she decided to come up with an excuse if he ever approached her for another dance. With a farewell flip of her hand, she took a few steps toward a chair and had to bite back a grimace of pain from her bruised feet, and tried not to limp. Hopefully the soreness would soon wear off.

An elderly lady took a seat in the chair Pamela was aiming for, so she headed for an alcove, where she could sit in peace. Once there, she unfurled her fan and waved it so the moving air would cool her cheeks, grateful to rest her aching feet and catch her breath.

With a flurry of blue silk skirts and the scent of roses, Elizabeth sat down beside her and let out a happy breath. "Good thing I spotted you heading here, else I would have searched for ages."

"No, you wouldn't have."

Elizabeth laughed and patted her hand. "You're right. I would have known you were hiding and tracked you down by peering into the alcoves and behind the palms or Doric columns."

As if I could fit behind a Doric column. Although Pamela had long since lost the childhood pudginess that had earned her the nickname of *Piggy* from her brothers, she still hadn't slimmed down enough to display a fashionably small waist. "The best place to find me is in the library," she strove for a light tone.

"As well I know. I will make you sit with me where everyone can see you," Elizabeth said, a good-natured warning.

"It won't do any good. You'll be gone in a minute, dancing with some man, and I'll sneak away again and hide."

Elizabeth wrinkled her nose. "We have such a crush here. Just think of the women and children we'll be able to help!" Her eyes sparkled as she scanned the ballroom.

"We can take on new families, perhaps as many as twenty," Pamela joined in her enthusiasm.

"Pay school fees for the older children!"

Pamela snapped her fan closed, relieved to see Elizabeth's eyes were free of sorrow, at least for a few minutes. Balls were especially hard on her. She and her fiancé Richard had met at one, and her friend had too many memories of laughing and dancing in his arms—of romantic happiness.

Richard's death, as well as the loss of Elizabeth's parents, had devastated her, causing a dark painful time. Because she was in mourning, she missed the social season two years ago, had barely participated last year, and had struggled through the first parties of this season. Tonight was the first occasion where Pamela had seen a return of Elizabeth's former liveliness.

Pamela wished a new man was the cause for her friend's good spirits. But she suspected Elizabeth was enjoying the success of the evening they'd both worked so hard to achieve.

"I thought you and Henry were going to collide with the second row of dancers."

"I declare, next time I dance with Henry…if I *ever* dance with Henry again…I'm going to lead."

Elizabeth let out a peal of laughter. "I don't think he would mind, poor dear."

Pamela chuckled. "He's such a good man as long as he's not on the dance floor."

Leaning close, Elizabeth raised her eyebrow. "You're using a very fond tone. After a dance like that, I would have been so exasperated. Have you decided to set your cap for Henry? He would make an amiable husband."

Pamela's good spirits deflated. If Elizabeth, the friend who knew the wishes of her heart, was urging her toward Henry, she must think that Pamela was on her last hope. *I'm already twenty-one, practically on the shelf.* "I'm fated to become an old maid."

"Nonsense!" Elizabeth straightened and shot a stern look at Pamela. Pink flooded her friend's cheeks, making her look even more striking.

"It's no use, Beth. I'm not beautiful and vivacious like you. Men don't *see* me. And with the setbacks to Papa's business and the loss of my dowry, no incentive exists for them to try."

"Stop that!" Elizabeth hissed. "Don't you *dare* disparage yourself in such a way!"

Pamela was taken aback by Elizabeth's unusual vehemence.

"Plenty of women aren't '*beautiful and vivacious.*' They still find husbands. And that means you can too!"

"I'm not like you, Beth," Pamela repeated, her fingers running over the edge of her fan.

"You don't have to be like *me*," Elizabeth said with an edge in her tone. "Be *yourself*. The person you are when we're together. When you are animated, Pam, you have your own prettiness. You just lack assurance of your worth. You must overcome your shyness. You need to smile more and talk with prospective suitors." Her tone softened. "Please, Pam, won't you at least try? Let them see your goodness, your intelligence, your many accomplishments."

"I have many?" Pamela asked in a joking tone.

Elizabeth refused to be sidetracked. "I know you want to fall in love and marry." The sadness returned to her eyes, and her shoulders drooped. "At least *one* of us needs to marry and have babies."

Guilt flooded Pamela for reminding Elizabeth of her loss.

"Oh, no," she protested, taking her friend's hand and squeezing. After Richard's death from influenza, everyone had rushed to reassure the grief-stricken young woman that she'd love again, as if her fiancé were someone she could just replace. Their comments, no matter how well meaning, had caused deep pain. But two years had passed. Now, Pamela dared to make the suggestion. "You'll fall in love again, Beth." She held her breath for her friend's reaction.

"I've had my chance," Elizabeth said with false gaiety. "The kind of love Richard and I shared comes once in a lifetime." She touched her chest, to the locket with his picture that she wore under her dress, and stroked a finger over the shape. "Now I will be an aunt to your children. Playing with your babies will make me happy."

Pamela wanted to cry at the thought. Elizabeth would make a wonderful wife and mother. But she held in the emotion. Too many tears had fallen over the last few years—from both of them.

"So, you must stop holding yourself back, Pam. Promise?"

"I'll try."

Elizabeth rolled her eyes. "I know about how you *try*, Pamela Marie Burke-Smythe. That's not good enough."

Relieved to hear Elizabeth sounding more like herself, Pamela hastened to agree. "I *will* do so." *If only for your sake.*

Thomas Fyffe, tall and thin like a stork, came up to where they sat. He bobbed a bow, politely greeting both women.

With stiff lips, Pamela practiced turning up her lips and tried to think of something to say. Normally, she wouldn't have any problems with smiling at the scholarly man, but the pressure of the promise she'd just made seemed to stifle her thoughts and curb her tongue.

Gesturing to the floor, he solicited Elizabeth for the next dance.

Her friend agreed and, as he whisked her away, she glanced over her shoulder at Pamela and gave her a speaking glance.

Pamela watched the couple waltz. She saw how Elizabeth stayed in serious conversation with Mr. Fyffe throughout the dance. The two were probably discussing Ancient Greece, a passion of his, even though Elizabeth didn't share the same interests.

Conversing with a man is difficult enough. Dancing and talking at the same time seems an impossible task.

Shame tightened her stomach. Despite her promise to Elizabeth, Pamela realized, *I can't do it.*

Standing in the foyer of the ballroom, John tugged at his collar, uncomfortable in his new evening clothes.

Regal Hester Burton, beauty still showing in the bones of her face, a tiara glittering on her snowy hair, reached up and touched his hand, exerting unspoken pressure for him to leave his collar alone. "You look very handsome, John."

"I don't know that you've put enough spit-and-polish on the cowboy."

"You are a *gentleman*, John," Great-Aunt Hester reproved. "You might not have the polish of the men here tonight, but I think that's all to the good."

He raised an eyebrow in question.

She patted his shoulder. "You're a western rancher, my dear boy. You need to look like who you are. For a young woman to make a transition from Boston to the new life you offer in the West will be difficult enough, worse if you misrepresent yourself."

"That's true."

"Come." She took his arm. "Time to meet the eligible young ladies of Boston."

Together, they walked into the ballroom. John's first impression was of warm, perfumed air, beautiful women in a rainbow of elegant gowns, and music from many instruments that enticed him into the enormous white room, bigger than his whole ranch house, which was probably the largest in Sweetwater Springs. He tried to hide his fascination with the carved panels, two-story arched windows with golden silk draperies, several marble fireplaces, the lofty gilded and carved ceiling.

John thought he'd been awestruck by Hester's mansion, but the Sofit mansion stunned him with the size and opulence of the ballroom.

Apparently taking the splendor in stride, his great-aunt steered him toward a couple and began introductions.

Before too long, John became overwhelmed in his attempt to juggle names and faces. The sophistication of the guests made him feel as if he didn't belong in their presence. No one discussed the breeding weight of their bulls, or the price of beef on the hoof, or that their horse needed shoeing. Fashion trends and gossip about people he didn't know seemed to be the topics at hand.

In the beginning of the evening, a few pretty women caught his attention, and he noticed a beautiful blonde in pale blue...until he saw three more young blondes in a similar color. Only moments later, he no longer recalled enough about the first one to describe her to Hester.

Soon the people began to blur together, and John gave up even trying to remember names. A quick glance around the crowded ballroom showed more people in one room than he suspected lived in the entire vicinity of Sweetwater Springs.

Hester had drifted a few feet away and looked to be discreetly flirting with a gentleman about her age.

John looked around for a place he could escape to for a few minutes. A curving staircase on one side of the room led to a balcony. No one stood at the railing, so he figured he might have the space to himself. On higher ground, he could do some reconnaissance, find his feet again before descending back into the fray.

Skirting the edge of the crowd, he moved to the stairway and began to climb. He reached the top and stood at the rail looking down. Away from the herd of people, he could enjoy the patterns of color the couples made as they twirled around the floor. Hester had hired a dancing instructor yesterday to give him some pointers, and he'd practiced with his great-aunt. But he'd rather plunge headfirst into an icy lake, face a grizzly bare-handed, or wrestle a panther to the ground than lead a young lady out on that dance floor and make a spectacle of himself for all eyes to see.

Soft footsteps, the rustle of skirts, and the scent of Lily of the Valley told him his great-aunt had followed him upstairs. "You've found a good observation post. I wouldn't have thought of it."

"Reconnaissance," he spoke aloud his earlier thought.

She laughed in delight. "Then by all means, we'll take advantage of our viewpoint." Her tone turned serious. "Let me give you some advice, my dear." Hester discretely gestured with her furled fan at one slender woman in a white gown. "Not her. She'll be charming to your face and catty behind your back. That one—" she indicated a pale redhead with a lift of her chin "—poor health." A shift of a shoulder directed his attention to a blonde in a green dress. "Empty-headed. You'll be bored in a week."

John let his gaze rove, stopping at another blonde.

Hester followed his glance. "No. She's a widow. I've nothing against a widow. But she never had children in two years of marriage. No sense taking the risk." She discreetly gestured toward another woman. "Mary is also a widow with a young daughter. I don't think you want to take on a little girl right now."

No, I already have my hands full with a grieving boy. I'd like my wife to concentrate solely on him. Thinking of Nick made John remember the urgency of his mission—of his need to find a bride and return home to the boy and his ranch.

"I'm not familiar with that clump of young ladies. Of course I know their names, but not their characters. I can make inquiries if one catches your attention."

None of the ladies stood out to him. "As you wish."

"Now there's whom I had in mind for you." Hester tipped her head toward a blonde in a pale blue dress. "Elizabeth Hamilton."

With a quickening of interest, he recognized the lady he'd admired earlier.

"A lovely woman, good family, intelligent, with quite a substantial dowry."

As owner of the largest ranch near Sweetwater Springs, John had thought he had plenty to offer a woman. But that was before he'd found out what Boston was really like. John doubted he had enough to entice such a woman.

"I do charity work with Miss Hamilton. Her parents died two years ago, leaving her and her brother a considerable fortune. He also has the business of course. Her fiancé also died at that time. No man has interested her since, although plenty have tried. Her face and fortune attract many."

Even as his gaze lingered on the beauty, John shook his head.

"Miss Hamilton would certainly understand your godson's pain. She has suffered similar losses, even though she was older at the time of her parents and fiancé's deaths."

"That is true, but I wouldn't want to compete with a former love. I want someone whose heart is open."

Hester gave him a sad smile. "I'm proof that a woman can love a second time after she loses her first husband." Her eyes took on a reminiscing glow. "After Albert died, I thought I'd take a broken heart to my grave. Edward taught me to love again. He was a completely different man, and we had a very different, but no less deeply loving, marriage."

That's what I want, he realized. *Deeply loving most perfectly describes my hopes for marriage.*

"I met Edward when I visited a friend in Boston. Being away

from New York…from the scene of my former happiness and my grief also helped me."

Perhaps I do have something to offer Miss Hamilton that she cannot obtain in Boston. His uncertainty must have shown on his face.

Great-Aunt Hester tapped her fan on the railing. "That girl was joyously in love with Richard. To see the shadow in her eyes since his death has saddened me. A change of scene, something besides charity work to occupy her mind and hands, a good man to warm her bed…. I think Elizabeth Hamilton will find herself falling in love with you. At least give her a chance, John."

He owed his Great-Aunt so much. How could he refuse her request?

Chapter Four

While Elizabeth danced with Mr. Fyffe, Pamela studied the people around her. On the right side, a tall man she didn't know—and she had the whole invitation list memorized—caught her attention. He was escorting elderly Mrs. Burton, a friend of her grandmother's and a *grand dame* of society, through the throng with a hand under her elbow. The pair made frequent stops for introductions along the way.

Curious, Pamela watched them, deciding she liked the look of the stranger. He had sandy hair, a craggy face, and a lanky build. Even though he was dressed in the same kind of evening attire as the rest of the male guests, something about him seemed different. Maybe his stance—more wide-legged than most men—or the air of strength about him.

The music ended, and Elizabeth cut across her view of Mrs. Burton and her companion.

"You haven't moved from this spot," her friend scolded, taking the chair next to her. "Is this how you keep your promise?" She leaned over and tucked tendrils of Pamela's hair, which had escaped the pins, back into her coiffure.

Pamela hated how her fine brown hair always failed to stay in place. Despite being indoors, she often ended up with a windblown appearance. "I've been watching everyone." Eager to divert her friend from another lecture and gain some information on the stranger, she tipped her head in the direction of Mrs. Burton. "Do you know that man?"

Elizabeth studied him, her forehead crinkled. "I've never seen him before." She turned to Pamela, speculation in her eyes. "Are you interested?"

"I'm curious. That's all. He's very solicitous of Mrs. Burton, which makes me think they must be related, but she has only daughters and granddaughters."

"They're heading this way, so we'll find out soon enough." Elizabeth tapped Pamela's leg. "Do dance with him if he asks."

Mrs. Burton and her companion drew close and stopped in front of them. The elderly woman gifted them with a regal nod and a smile. "Miss Hamilton, Miss Burke-Smythe, this is my great-nephew, John Carter."

I was right. He is a relative.

"He has a vast ranch in Montana Territory and is here for a short visit." Although Mrs. Burton addressed both of them, she focused more on Elizabeth.

Elizabeth and Pamela returned her greeting.

The corners of Mr. Carter's blue eyes crinkled when he smiled. He made a gesture toward his head, as if he meant to tip a nonexistent hat, then quickly lowered his hand.

Mrs. Burton gestured toward Pamela. "Miss Burke-Smythe, I haven't seen your father here. No doubt he's avoiding the festivities."

"No doubt at all," Pamela echoed with a nod. "He's at home, probably in his favorite old chair in front of the fire in the library, reading. He made a donation to the society, and no amount of persuasion would budge him from his declaration not to attend tonight. Even Elizabeth tried to work her wiles on him, but to no avail."

"Newton always was a stubborn man with a dislike of society gatherings. His mother despaired of him ever marrying."

"I can understand his predilection," Pamela said shyly. "Many a night I join him in the other leather chair in front of the fireplace, companionably reading, while my brothers are out on their various entertainments."

Mr. Carter eyed her with interest, his eyebrow cocked.

She blushed and glanced at her fingers.

A new set of music struck up. Another waltz.

Mrs. Burton tapped Mr. Carter on the back of his arm with her closed fan, as if urging him forward. "It's customary to ask a young lady to dance, my dear boy," she said in a humorous tone. "I'm sure Miss Hamilton will oblige you."

Pamela couldn't help wishing that, for just this once, she'd been the one chosen over Elizabeth. But why should she be? Elizabeth was prettier, more charming, had a big dowry—all qualities which would make her the obvious choice for a matchmaking great-aunt.

John shot Hester a wry smile, placed a hand on his chest, and dipped a slight bow. "Please take pity on me, Miss Hamilton. Remember, I'm from Montana Territory, and not familiar with ballroom dancing." He made a self-depreciating grimace.

Pamela liked his voice, rich with a hint of a Western twang, as well as his lack of arrogance. Not many men would admit to their short-comings.

Mr. Carter's eyes twinkled at Elizabeth. "I'll do my best not to step on you or lead you astray," he drawled in a teasing manner.

His words made Pamela remember Henry. She exchanged amused glances with Elizabeth. *Now it's her turn to have her toes trod upon.* She didn't allow her amusement to show. Mr. Carter seemed completely comfortable in this environment, but she sensed that underneath he was uncertain, which gave her a feeling of kinship with him.

As she watched John lead Elizabeth toward the dance floor, Pamela bit her lip to repress an unexpected sense of yearning and an odd feeling of jealousy. *I want to dance with the Western rancher.*

While she'd envied her friend her popularity, Pamela had

never before felt proprietary about a specific suitor of Elizabeth's. Experiencing the emotion made her feel ashamed for even thinking such uncharitable thoughts, especially about someone so dear to her and who had suffered so much in the last few years.

Mrs. Burton spread her fan open and languidly waved it, wafting Lily of the Valley fragrance Pamela's way. "I'm pleased to see Miss Hamilton looking more like her old self."

Astonished at Mrs. Burton's perception, Pamela turned to face the older woman. "I was thinking the same thing earlier."

"But I still sometimes see sadness in her eyes."

Pamela gave Mrs. Burton a thoughtful glance, seeing the shrewdness in the woman's faded blue eyes. "Most people don't notice. I doubt even her brother knows how much Elizabeth still struggles to keep up her spirits."

"My great-nephew would be a good match for Miss Hamilton," Mrs. Burton said, with her characteristic bluntness. "He'll take her away from the place of her painful memories, give her new challenges to occupy her mind and her time. Your friend has plenty of backbone. I think she'll thrive in the West."

With a sinking heart, Pamela realized Mrs. Burton was right. She glanced at the couple. Mr. Carter wasn't a polished dancer, but she suspected he hadn't much practice. At least he guided his partner in the right direction, unlike poor Henry. Her friend seemed animated, and from this distance, it was difficult to know if Elizabeth was just being mannerly and trying to put the Western man at ease, or if she truly was interested in him as a potential suitor.

Mrs. Burton gave a nod of obvious satisfaction. "They look well together."

They do. The thought wrenched at Pamela's heart. "I couldn't bear for her to travel so far from Boston. I'd never see her, and we are so very close." Life would be lonely without Elizabeth. She had other friends, but none so dear.

But I've prayed every night that Beth would find happiness again. What if Mr. Carter is the answer to my persistent petitions to the Almighty?

Pamela bit her lip, then voiced her thoughts. "But if Elizabeth could find happiness...true happiness and love...I would wholeheartedly endorse the idea of her marrying Mr. Carter and moving West."

Mrs. Burton gave Pamela a shrewd look. "That's very charitable of you."

"I love her," Pamela said simply. "When you love someone, you want the best for them. If I could know Elizabeth can once again experience joy...." She placed a hand on her chest and blinked at the stinging in her eyes. "Why, that would mean more to me than my own sadness over losing her."

"You two have been bosom friends for a long time," Mrs. Burton said, a sympathetic expression on her face. "Even distance, living separate lives, doesn't break that kind of connection."

"You are wise, Mrs. Burton." Pamela forced a smile. "We could always write letters," she said, trying to sound optimistic when she felt just the opposite.

"A regular correspondence can be a godsend. Pouring out your heart, your intimate thoughts to a beloved friend—such confidences are good for the soul."

Pamela nodded. *But not as good as talking face to face about such matters.*

Mrs. Burton's lips trembled before she firmed them. "I moved away from my best friend, and we continued to correspond with one another...oh, at least several times a month until her death a few years ago."

"I'm sorry you lost her."

Mrs. Burton snapped her fan shut, obviously wanting to avoid sentiment. "I see no reason why we can't put our heads together and make a match between them."

If Elizabeth wishes to wed Mr. Carter, how can I not?

"We can call upon Miss Hamilton," Mrs. Burton mused. "And there are several dinner parties to attend this week, as well as the Spencer ball. I think you and Miss Hamilton should join my great-nephew and I on some sightseeing trips around the city."

"Those are good places to start," Pamela agreed, not entirely truthfully, then thought, *do I really want to promote such a marriage?*

As the beautiful Elizabeth Hamilton placed her hand on his arm, and they walked onto the dance floor, John wondered why he wasn't moved by her touch—if he should feel something besides nervousness—excitement perhaps? Pride at escorting such a lovely woman? Anticipation? *Maybe, the idea of dancing in front of so many people is disguising anything else I might be feeling.*

John glanced at Great-Aunt Hester and saw her in serious conversation with Miss... *What is her name again? Something hyphenated.*

The young woman, plain and unobtrusive, who liked quiet nights reading, watched them. *Is that yearning in her brown eyes?* She caught his glance and looked away.

The expression on her plump-cheeked face lingered in his mind, and John wondered what she was feeling. *Did she want to dance?*

I'll ask her next, he promised himself.

The music began—a sweet thrum of stringed instruments that made him wish he could just sit and listen, not have to talk to a herd of elegant strangers or dance with a lady whose beauty and grace made him feel as if he had two left feet. He gave Miss Hamilton a perfunctory smile, inhaling her rose perfume.

"Have you danced much, Mr. Carter?"

"A harvest celebration or two." John thought of the fast-paced reels, hops, and polkas favored by the Westerners. "Not like this." He fell silent, listening for the beat and trying to remember everything he'd learned from his lesson yesterday. *One two three, one two three...*

How strange to glide across the floor holding a woman, his hand on her waist, feeling the ribs of her corset under his palm. Even through his gloves, the material of her gown felt light and slippery. He was grateful his rough hands were covered so they wouldn't snag the delicate fabric. John swept Miss Hamilton into the first wide turn, keeping an eye on the couples nearest them, and thought about cutting a calf from the herd. *Couldn't be much more difficult than that.*

He'd been riding and roping since he was three years old. He'd only been waltzing since yesterday. A young couple bobbled toward them, and with a long step, he shifted Miss Hamilton to the side, hoping she thought he was guiding, not pushing, her out of the way.

Another pair drifted by in earnest discussion. John hoped Miss Hamilton wouldn't expect him to talk. He was too preoccupied with counting. *One two three, one two three...*

"*Das Leben ein Tanz,*" she quoted.

John restrained a start of panic. A conversation in a foreign language was definitely more than he could manage, even if he weren't waltzing.

"The Dance of Life. This music was composed by Johan Strauss."

John wished he could mop his damp brow. At least, Miss Hamilton had switched to English and didn't seem to expect a response. He nodded.

"Tell me about your ranch, Mr. Carter."

She does want me to talk and dance. He waited a few more measures, until they had moved away from the obstacles onto a clear stretch of floor, before answering her. "Biggest spread in the area." *There!* He'd managed words and dance steps at the same time.

She raised one eyebrow. "Spread?"

"Ranch," John pushed out, concentrating. He risked a glance over to the orchestra. *Would this waltz ever end?*

The loss of concentration almost led to disaster. He narrowly avoided plowing into a couple who'd slowed in front of them. Hopefully his partner hadn't noticed.

John brought his attention back to Miss Hamilton, who gazed at him in expectancy. *What does she want from me?*

A trickle of sweat raced down his back. *The process of cutting a potential wife from the herd was proving far more difficult than he'd thought.*

Wistfully, Pamela watched Mr. Carter and Elizabeth finish the waltz. As he escorted his partner back toward Pamela and Mrs. Burton, a flicker of relief crossed his face, and she wondered why. Surely he would have wished for more time with Elizabeth. After a dance, most men tried to keep her talking, lingering on the edge of the floor instead of walking her back right away like they always did with Pamela.

As the two approached, they continued a conversation they'd obviously started earlier. "My grandparents lived in a log cabin." Mr. Carter flicked his hand to indicate their surroundings. "I can't even imagine how difficult they must have found such a primitive home after living a more genteel life."

"Difficult, indeed," Mrs. Burton said. "I remember my sister Olivia's letters of complaint. But those two were deeply in love and determined to make a new life in the West for themselves away from their families." Her eyes held a look of old sadness. "Our father was, well, overbearing. Quite a tyrant. He had someone already picked out for Olivia. A business partner. The only way the young lovers could marry was to run away."

Mr. Carter shot his great-aunt a curious look. "I didn't know that about my grandparents. But then again, I was a little shaver when they passed away."

"That's a romantic story," Pamela commented, hoping her wistful tone went unnoticed.

Elizabeth wrinkled her nose. "Oh, I don't know. Hardships and difficulties don't sound romantic to me."

"In this case, Miss Burke-Smythe and I are in agreement." Mrs. Burton slid her gaze to Elizabeth. "Olivia and John had a good life, despite the hardships. They found happiness. In spite of her occasional complaints, Olivia's letters were full of pride in their accomplishments."

Miss Hamilton's gaze roved the crowd. "Do you live in a log cabin, Mr. Carter?" she asked absently.

Pamela found the conversation fascinating and couldn't understand how Elizabeth allowed her attention to wander, as if casting for other partners.

Mr. Carter's eyebrows drew together. "I assure you, my home is not so primitive. Simple, perhaps, compared to this. A two-story home. Five bedrooms."

Sounds promising. But would Elizabeth think so? Her friend wasn't looking convinced.

Elizabeth waved to a swain.

Mr. Carter didn't seem to mind. He bowed to Pamela. "May I have this dance?"

With a flip of her heart, she smiled and nodded, rising to her feet.

He crooked his elbow toward her.

Pamela slipped her hand around his arm, feeling the hard muscle under her palm. Although Mr. Carter was an obvious gentleman, he also worked outside, not in a business office behind a desk. Thinking about his muscles gave her a flutter in her stomach.

As they walked toward the dance floor, Pamela barely felt the bruises on her feet from Henry. The thrill of waltzing with Mr. Carter practically banished the ache.

On the floor, he took her into his arms. She liked the feel of his hand on her waist, the press of their gloved palms together. For the first time, the intimate posture, which had always made her feel uncomfortable and stiff, seemed right, and she wished he would pull her closer.

Throughout the beginning of the waltz, they remained silent. She had the sense that Mr. Carter was concentrating on his steps, and she didn't want to distract him.

He frowned. "I'm sorry I'm not a very good dancer."

"Not at all." Pamela thought of Henry and had to restrain a laugh. She didn't want Mr. Carter to think she was making fun of him. "You couldn't possibly be worse than my previous partner, who led me in the wrong direction *and* trod on my toes!"

His troubled expression cleared. "Well, then, I'm grateful you decided to risk your toes again with me. I promise, I'll try to keep my boots on the floor where they belong." He wiggled his eyebrows.

Pamela laughed at his playful act. "I watched you with Elizabeth, and you were fine. So accepting your invitation to dance was not such a risk as you're making it out to be."

As they bantered, Pamela found herself relaxing. Conversing with this stranger she'd only met twenty minutes ago was far easier than talking with some men she'd known all her life.

Mr. Carter also seemed to become comfortable. His lead became more expert, and he picked up their speed. As they became in tune with each other, they flowed in perfect step to the music. Exhilaration welled up in Pamela. She'd never known dancing could feel like this.

She glanced up at him, feeling a smile as wide as the moon stretch across her face. "We're flying!"

An answering gleam of laughter sparked in his eyes, and he grinned. "Soaring, indeed."

She liked the crinkle of laugh lines around his mouth.

The music ended with a flourish, and Pamela settled back to earth, disappointed the waltz was over—an unknown experience. In the past, she'd always been glad to escape her partner. *I've never danced with the right man.*

Pamela forced herself to set aside the surprising thought. But Mr. Carter, like every other available man at the ball, probably had his eyes set on Elizabeth. Soon this evening, and especially this dance, would only be a memory.

He grinned as he gazed downward. "I managed to protect your toes."

"My feet and I thank you, kind sir." Pamela smiled up at him. *Did I really just use a flirtatious tone?* "I've never enjoyed a dance more."

Mr. Carter cocked his eyebrow. "I think you're pulling my leg, trying to make this greenhorn feel good," he drawled.

"No. Well, yes, of course I'd like you to feel comfortable." Pamela's cheeks grew hot. "But that's not why I said so. It's the truth."

"That's mighty kind of you." His gaze dropped to her lips. "I enjoyed our dance, too," he said in a more serious tone. "You have my thanks for making me feel at ease." He guided her back to her seat, where Elizabeth and Mrs. Burton stood in conversation.

Elizabeth beamed and leaned closer. "You looked very poised out there," she said quietly.

"It felt so natural," she whispered so no one else could hear. She wished she could say so out loud. But if Pamela expressed any interest in the man as a suitor, she knew Elizabeth would draw back from him, wanting to give her friend a clear field.

The music struck up for the next set. Strains of "The Blue Danube" floated to them—Richard's favorite waltz.

Elizabeth whitened, a stricken look in her eyes. She pasted on a smile, tilted up her chin.

Seeing her friend put a brave face on her pain made Pamela's heart ache and firmed her determination.

Elizabeth needs what Mr. Carter has to offer far more than I do.

Chapter Five

Three days later, John and Hester sat in the *calèche*, a fashionable open-air carriage belonging to Great-Aunt Hester, across from Miss Hamilton and Miss Burke-Smythe, taking in the sights of Boston. The day was warm and breezy for the beginning of May, with a hint of the briny ocean, which he had yet to see.

They'd driven through busy parts of the city, where he'd been dismayed by the volume of traffic—big horse-drawn omnibuses, hacks with the cabbies yelling out their availability, wagons full of merchandise, and elegant private carriages clattering over the cobbles. Men, boys, and sometimes even a woman pushed hand-held two-wheeled carts. Not even the piles of manure softened the noise of hoofbeats. Adults had to make their way more carefully around the stinking clumps.

Urchins darted across the streets through the two-way flow of vehicles, and John winced when he saw a boy almost run over by a swift hack.

He was relieved when their driver steered the horses to a quieter thoroughfare lined by brick buildings with windows trimmed in white. But as interesting as his surroundings, John was more fascinated by the young ladies in the calèche with him.

Both wore straw bonnets with silken ribbons that matched their dresses, pale blue for Miss Hamilton, buttercup yellow for Miss Burke-Smythe. If he'd driven with the three ladies down the main street of Sweetwater Springs in this equipage, he'd have been the envy of every bachelor. Even his great-aunt's white hair wouldn't be a deterrent to the old geezers who sought a wife.

In spite of three days of afternoon calls and nights of dinner parties, John felt he had yet to get a handle on Elizabeth Hamilton's true character. Yes, she was beautiful, intelligent, and educated, with an outward poise and gaiety that belied the sadness he sometimes saw flash in her eyes. But he hadn't reached an understanding of the inner woman.

This quest for a bride was proving far more difficult than he'd thought. Already a week had passed since he'd been gone. Worries about the ranch...wondering how everyone, especially Nick, fared in his absence, nagged at him. John wanted to return home. But he couldn't possibly marry someone whose character he couldn't discern. Even more important than his own marital contentment was Nick's well-being, and he wanted to feel more sure of his future wife.

He hadn't yet ventured to talk to Miss Hamilton about the death of her fiancé. Sometimes, the man's presence seemed so strong as if he was a specter traveling with them. While John could understand and respect her grief, he didn't want a ghost following the newlyweds to Montana.

Nor had John had a chance to tell Miss Hamilton about Nick. He hoped her losses would make her understand and empathize with Nick. *Today*, he promised himself. *I'll bring up the topic.*

He glanced at the other young lady. Pamela Burke-Smythe was far more quiet than her friend, seldom speaking unless addressed. Yet her thoughts often flitted across her face, giving him more insight into her character than Miss Hamilton, with all her vivacity and conversation had revealed.

The carriage pulled to a stop in front of Christ Church, better known as the old North Church. Gazing at the Georgian style structure in awe, John was able to temporarily set aside his worries and become lost in history.

Elizabeth waved her hand at the steeple. "There you have it,

Mr. Carter. The very place where the lantern was lit to signal the British were coming by land or sea."

John shaded his eyes and glanced upward.

"The steeple was the tallest in Boston," Elizabeth instructed. "The bells within were the first ones brought to America. Paul Revere was one of the bell ringers."

He shook his head. "Such rich history."

His great-aunt inclined her head in agreement. "One of our ancestors participated in the famous Boston tea party, John. I have his journal in my library. You may read it while you are here."

"I'd heard the story, but I'd love to read the account." When he thought of the bravery of his forefathers and of how ill-equipped the revolutionaries were to face the mighty British empire, John couldn't help the tingle of awe racing down his spine.

"Listen, my children, and you shall hear…" Pamela Burke-Smythe quoted in a soft tone.

John looked at her with speculation. Miss Burke-Smythe seldom spoke without being asked a question or nudged by her friend, but when she did, he always found her interesting. "Of the midnight ride of Paul Revere," he added.

Miss Hamilton opened her mouth as if to join in, then pressed her lips together, a gleam in her eyes when she glanced from her friend to him.

While Great-Aunt Hester and Miss Hamilton looked on in obvious amusement, he and Miss Burke-Smythe took turns reciting the rest of Longfellow's poem. When they finished, their eyes met and held, obviously feeling in perfect accord.

Miss Hamilton clapped her hands together. "I remember when our governess made us memorize that," she told John. "Living next door and being friends made our parents decide Pamela and I could share a governess." She wrinkled her nose at her friend. "You always like poetry better than I, Pam. And Mr. Carter, you seem to as well?"

"On long horseback rides mentally reciting poems passes the time or keeps me alert. Robert Burns is a particular favorite of mine. Also William Wordsworth."

"Oh, yes! I like both of those poets," Miss Burke-Smythe exclaimed, her hands clasped in front of her chest.

"Whom else?" he asked her.

"Emily Dickinson. Elizabeth Barrett Browning."

"She walks in beauty like the night, of cloudless climes and starry skies." As John spoke the lines, he should have looked at Miss Hamilton, who was the personification of the poet's words. But he found himself drawn by the flush of pink in Miss Burke-Smythe's cheeks, which gave her a quiet prettiness.

"You quite surprise me, Mr. Carter." Miss Hamilton raised her eyebrows. "From the stories I've read of the West, I never would have thought cowboys liked poetry."

"Not all do, of course. But the scenery of Montana Territory can be the inspiration for the mind and heart…the arching blue sky, rushing rivers, forested mountains, the prairie grasses swaying in the wind. Poetry in nature."

As she listened, Miss Burke-Smythe's lips parted, and her brown eyes sparkled as if her imagination caught the images he described.

As much as he enjoyed the conversation about poetry, John had a mission for today. He wrenched his thoughts back to what he wanted to discuss with Miss Hamilton. This seemed like a perfect introduction to the difficult topic. "I have nine cowboys who work for me, most of them uneducated. But they like being read to. And I have one boy, my thirteen-year-old godson, who's lately come into my charge." He launched into an explanation about Nick. As John told the story of the Sanders's deaths, he watched Miss Burke-Smythe's expression softened with sympathy.

She leaned forward, and her fingers moved as if she wanted to reach out to him.

Although Miss Hamilton wore an expression of polite interest, she grew quiet. Her fingers toyed with the locket hanging from a gold chain around her neck. She held herself rigid, pressing back against the seat as if to distance herself from the conversation.

No, John realized. *She was trying to escape the pain his revelation of Nick's circumstances made her feel.*

In that moment, John realized he'd been courting the wrong woman. Elizabeth Hamilton's sadness was still too strong, her pain too raw. If hearing about the Sanders's accident made her react in such a way, how would she respond to the reality of his grieving godson? The boy was too sensitive not to feel her withdraw around him.

Realizing he'd just lost the focus of his courtship, John floundered to silence. *I'll have to start all over.* Frustration spiked through him at the thought of riding through the herd of debutantes, searching for someone special. *I cannot delay my return.*

Miss Burke-Smythe pressed a hand to her chest. "I feel for the poor boy. To lose his family in such a manner. I remember when my little sister died." She glanced at Elizabeth, but her friend looked away. "She was three, almost four. We mourned..." her voice hitched, and she swallowed. "Sometimes, I think of Mary and miss her still."

I, too, lost a younger sister. John's throat closed on the old pain and guilt. He never spoke of Sarah.

Miss Burke-Smythe's gaze held compassion. "How long ago did the Sanders's accident take place?"

"Six months."

"Not much time at all," she commented. "You must also be mourning for them."

"Yes." One stark word conveyed his strong feelings.

"How is Nick doing?" Miss Burke-Smythe asked.

"He's quiet, keeps to himself." John shook his head in dismay.

"Boys aren't supposed to be quiet!" Miss Burke-Smythe exchanged another glance with her friend.

This time, Miss Hamilton gave a slight nod of agreement and pulled her lips into a faint smile. "We are far too familiar with boys. Between the two of us, having four brothers, pests that they were...."

"And sometimes still are," Miss Burke-Smythe said with humor.

A reminiscent expression crossed his great-aunt's face. "I had pesky brothers, too. It's something about the male species that never changes." They all laughed, as if relieved to lighten the painful subject.

Miss Burke-Smythe reached as if to touch John's knee but pulled back her hand. "Tell us more about Nick. What are his interests?"

As if peering through the spyglass that had belonged to a seafaring ancestor, John's blurry focus became clear. He'd not only spent these last three days with Miss Hamilton, but also with Miss Burke-Smythe. The shy woman's natural sympathy appealed to him, and he realized that, all along, he'd felt far more comfortable with her than with her more elegant friend.

His first reaction of overwhelming relief was soon tempered by uncertainty. John believed he had something to offer Miss Hamilton—an escape from her painful memories. With several brief glances, he studied the fine fabric of Miss Burke-Smythe's dress, the gold cross around her neck. She also came from a wealthy family. Why would she want to leave everyone she loved and go live in the West? He struggled to remember her question. Something about Nick's interests.

"The boy's good with horses," he said slowly, pondering his answer. "Has a gentle way with them." John had to think what else. Nick had dutifully studied his lessons, but he didn't seem to have a favorite subject in school. "He reads."

"We have some good bookstores in Boston if you want to purchase a selection of books to take home with you," Miss Burke-Smythe suggested.

"Good idea..." He'd almost slipped and said her given name, which is how he'd quickly come to think of her, something which had never happened with *Miss Hamilton*. "May I call you Pamela..." He glanced at her friend. "And Elizabeth?"

Both women smiled and nodded.

His aunt gave him a faint nod, a look of approval in her eyes. "Tell us more about what the boy might like."

"Music," he suddenly recalled. "One of my men has an old, battered fiddle. He let Nick play around with it. The boy's quite gifted. Has even composed a song or two. His parents mentioned they would buy him a violin for Christmas." John's voice trailed off, realizing that one of the reasons for that fateful trip to town must have been to order the instrument, and his stomach knotted. He forced himself to continue talking. "Now that I think of it, Nick hasn't picked up the fiddle since."

"We have a superb music shop in Boston," Pamela said, flashing a wide smile. "Instruments and sheets of music. Perhaps you should consider purchasing a violin for him."

John slapped his leg, delighted with the idea. "Now why didn't I think of that?"

"Should we stop by today?" Pamela glanced at Elizabeth. "You're on good terms with the owner."

Her friend nodded, seemingly relieved by the change in conversation. "I'm in that shop at least once a month, browsing for new music."

Instinctively, John knew buying an instrument for Nick was a good decision. Some of the tight anxiety he'd carried around for months eased with the idea of doing something constructive for his godson—something he felt in his gut the boy would respond to. He smiled at the ladies who waited for his answer. "Then that's settled. Let's go to the music store and buy Nick a violin."

After a day of shopping, the driver of Mrs. Burton's *calèche* took them home. Pamela was saddened to have their outing come to an end. John's appreciation for her advice about Nick had filled her with elation that made her feel more composed and confident in his presence, leading to the most enjoyable time she'd ever spent with a man.

The carriage was filled with parcels, with many more to be delivered in the next few days, and others already sent to Montana Territory. After stopping at the music shop for a violin and sheet music, they'd left Elizabeth to linger over choosing some music for herself, while Mrs. Burton, John, and Pamela had walked to the next building and into the bookstore.

There Pamela had delighted in sharing some of her favorite authors and volumes of poetry with John, as well as guiding him to some books favored by her brothers when they'd been younger. By the time they'd finished, they'd procured enough books to fill a crate. John arranged to ship them to Sweetwater Springs.

"So many presents. This will be the best homecoming." John glanced back at the pile of books on the counter. "We'll have enough reading material to keep us occupied for the next several winters."

Mrs. Burton slipped her hand around her great-nephew's arm. "The haberdashery next, my dear boy. If Nick's wardrobe is anything like yours was...."

"Probably worse. He's been shooting up like a weed and showing bony wrists under too-short sleeves."

At the men's emporium, they teased John into buying a new suit and several shirts for himself, as well as pants, shirts, a jacket, and undergarments for Nick. With much laughter and guesswork, John selected a new shirt for each of his cowboys. "I'm going to be the most popular boss around for miles," he joked.

They'd retrieved Elizabeth and next ventured to the shoemaker's, where John commissioned a pair of shoes and riding boots, as well as shoes and boots for Nick.

As they shopped, Pamela wondered if Nick would take boyish

delight in his presents, or if his sadness would overshadow the gifts. *Probably a bit of both.*

She'd so enjoyed helping John choose his purchases. Even Elizabeth had shaken off her earlier melancholy and joined in their enthusiasm. John had no choice but to be carried along in their wake.

Before heading home, they ended up celebrating their successes at the ice cream shop.

Their driver drew the carriage to a stop between hers and Elizabeth's houses, both large mansions that flanked each other on the street. Small front gardens led to three-story structures that were far longer than they were wide and contained formal gardens in the back.

John helped the two ladies out of the *calèche.* He smiled at Pamela, his gaze warm, and pressed her hand.

Her heart fluttered. Was it just her imagination, or had John lingered the slightest bit with her? She waved goodbye to her friend.

Elizabeth caught her arm to halt her. "Come inside with me for a moment."

Curious, Pamela followed her into the house. The butler greeted them, and a maid took Elizabeth's parcel of sheet music from her. They crossed the black-and-white tiled floor of the entryway and entered the parlor, where lilies blooming in a crystal vase perfumed the air. A few months ago, Elizabeth had redecorated the room in soothing blues and silver, claiming to want a more fashionable look, but really, Pamela suspected, attempting to erase the painful memories the parlor contained.

She waved Pamela to the sofa and took a seat in her favorite chair. "What do you think of John Carter?"

Elizabeth's casual tone didn't fool Pamela. Her friend only spoke in such a way when she was trying to be subtle about her quest for information.

"I like him very well, indeed." Heat flooded her cheeks, and she hoped Elizabeth didn't notice the telltale color.

"Too bad he doesn't live in Boston. I don't suppose we could persuade him to move?" Elizabeth shot Pamela an assessing glance. "He's a good man. I think he'd make a fine husband."

"I believe so, as well." She strove to keep her voice from trembling. "As we spend time with him, I like him more and more. But what about moving to Montana Territory?"

Elizabeth smiled. "Sounds like an adventure. Marriage to a man like John Carter would have many…*benefits.*" She tapped her chin with one finger. "But the thought of Nick troubles me."

Pamela felt a surge of sympathy for the boy. "He's at that uncertain age between child and man. He still needs maternal love, not that he'd admit it."

"And food," Elizabeth joked. "Remember how much the boys ate at that age?"

A knock sounded.

"Come in," Elizabeth called.

A maid entered the parlor, carrying a laden tray. The scent of tea and fresh baked cookies followed her into the room. She set the tray on the small table in front of the settee and left.

"Not for me." Pamela rose. "I need to be getting home. I want to rest before the Harte's party tonight." She motioned for her friend to stay seated. "You sit and have your tea."

But Elizabeth stood and unexpectedly hugged Pamela, before releasing her. "I'll see you tonight."

With a lump in her throat, Pamela hurried out of the room, knowing her friend was also anticipating a future where they would be separated. And not just by the miles. *When Beth marries John, she will be a wife and eventually, a mother. I'll remain an old maid.* She bit her lip to hold in the sadness.

Chapter Six

Three days later, John strode up to the door of the Burke-Smythe residence, hoping he wouldn't find Pamela's father or brothers at home. He wanted to spend some time alone with her—see if she'd consider the idea of marrying a rancher—before he formally approached her father to ask for his daughter's hand.

He'd spent the last days keeping company with Pamela, chaperoned by his great-aunt and always shadowed by Elizabeth. Now that John had turned his focus on Pamela, he wondered how he could have missed the fact that she was a much better match for him than her friend.

Hester concurred with his decision. She, too, had noticed Elizabeth's reaction to the news of Nick's bereavement. At first, his great-aunt had thought to keep searching for suitable brides, informing John of the loss of the Burke-Smythe fortune—warning that the most Pamela would bring to the marriage was a meager dowry. Once he explained to her that he didn't care about money, Hester became a strong supporter of his courtship.

Since that time, Great-Aunt Hester had seized any opportunity to engage Elizabeth in conversation, giving John and Pamela the illusion of privacy. Like a flower unfolding delicate petals, as she'd grown more comfortable with him, she'd lost her shyness and become more open. Making her smile warmed his insides, and he delighted in their conversations. They spoke of poetry, of Pamela's charity work, of his childhood on the ranch. He even shared stories about Andrew—something John thought he'd never do—surprised he could remember his friend with laughter.

Today, Hester had somehow ascertained Elizabeth was otherwise engaged, leaving Pamela free for the afternoon. His great-aunt had come up with the idea of John inviting the young woman for a drive to the harbor. She'd even offered to lend him her carriage. He'd chosen the surrey over the *calèche*, not wanting a driver, and knowing the smaller seating space would feel more intimate.

At the Burke-Smythe mansion, a handsome brick edifice more down-at-heel than the Hamilton place, a maid answered his knock and ushered him inside. In the last week, he'd become familiar with the Burke-Smythe abode. It wasn't quite as large as the Hamilton or Burton homes, and the furnishings were more comfortable, and even on the shabby side, than the other houses he'd visited.

The maid escorted him to the open door of the library, where he found Pamela sitting in a leather chair in a beam of sunlight from a nearby window. Normally, he would have focused on the books lining the floor-to-ceiling shelves—a grand wealth of volumes. Probably the whole number of books in Sweetwater Springs wouldn't fill up these library shelves. Now, instead of searching out titles, dipping into the pages, delighting in the discovery of some musty classic, his gaze was drawn to Pamela.

Dressed in a white shirtwaist and brown skirt, she had a gray kitten curled on her lap. With her head bent over her darning, she didn't immediately notice him.

He watched her deft fingers industriously ply the needle and wool thread through the heel of the black stocking, wondering why she was doing the housewifely chore, instead of leaving the task to a maid or sewing woman.

I have plenty of stockings that need darning.

Dora had been the one responsible for keeping the men's clothes clean and stockings darned. Since her death, they'd all taken on a disheveled look. Remembering her, familiar sadness rolled over him. But for the first time, the sharpness of the emotion was tempered by thoughts of Pamela putting to rights his clothes, his home, his grieving godson, and perhaps even his aching heart.

The kitten stretched and looked at him with sleepy golden eyes. Yawning, the small animal exposed sharp teeth and a tiny pink tongue.

Sensing him, Pamela looked up, and her eyes widened. "Mr. Carter." She hurriedly rolled the sock around a darning egg and tucked it inside a basket. She picked up the kitten, rose, and set the critter back on the chair, where it mewed in protest. "Stay here, Smoky." With a gentle touch, she patted the kitten's head before walking over to John. "I wasn't expecting visitors." She peered around him, as if looking for Hester.

"I've come to see if you'd like to go for a drive. I haven't yet seen the ocean, and I cannot return to Montana Territory without doing so. My Great-Aunt Hester assures me it is perfectly proper to ask you to accompany me."

"I'd love to. Let me send someone to ask Elizabeth if she's free to go with us."

"Great-Aunt Hester told me that Elizabeth was already engaged for the afternoon."

"Oh." An adorable expression of confusion came over her face. "But wouldn't you rather wait for another occasion when Elizabeth can come too?"

He chose his words carefully, knowing her shyness might make her draw back. "The sun is shining, and it's beautiful outside. I don't have much time left in Boston, and so I need to make the most of each day."

Her hand crept to her throat to finger a bit of lace on her shirtwaist.

"Please, Pamela," John coaxed, with a smile. "I don't have many friends in Boston, and I'd like to have someone to share my first sight of the ocean—someone who'd appreciate my sentiments."

"Why, of course." Pamela lowered her hand. "I'd be honored to accompany you, Mr. Carter. Let me run upstairs for my bonnet and a shawl." She hastened out of the room.

Once they were outside, John handed her into the surrey. He needed to stay alert—concentrate on his driving, so they headed toward the ocean in silence. Bad enough his unfamiliarity with the city and the crowded streets, but he didn't know the horse. Probably the gray would be fine, but he missed having his own horseflesh whose foibles he knew.

"Head toward State Street." Pamela smiled and indicated the direction she wanted to go. "See that huge building?" She pointed toward a massive six story structure, clad in rough granite. "Long Wharf is there."

John headed the horse toward the largest building he'd ever seen.

Pamela directed him to an area where they'd have a clear view of the harbor, with the many masted ships moored at the wharf or anchored farther out in the water. Longboats hauled sailors from their vessels to the land. The dock was crowded with stevedores unloading their ship's cargo. Sailors were distinguished by their rolling gait. Porters pushed carts full of goods, and other individuals whose purpose John couldn't discern bustled about.

He breathed in the briny smells, caught a whiff of fish, and felt the caress of the wind, somehow different from the same invisible force that moved through the air of Montana Territory. But most of all, he tried to look his fill at the expanse of olive green water, to impress upon his senses the memory of the scene before him.

John could feel Pamela stealing glances at his face, obviously wondering what he was thinking.

Finally, she couldn't seem to stand the suspense any longer. She grasped the ends of her shawl and leaned forward. "Is it as you imagined, Mr. Carter? The harbor, the ships?"

John glanced down at her. "'I never saw a Moor—I never saw the Sea...'"

"Emily Dickenson." Her eyes lit up. "'Yet know I how the heather looks, and what a billow be,'" she finished. "So it is, then?"

"Yes," he agreed, happy she knew the poem. "But not the vastness." John pointed straight ahead. "Where the edge hits the horizon." He shaded his eyes, scanning the area. "But I also didn't imagine so many ships."

"Ships from all over the world come here," she said with a proud tone.

"Stirs the imagination."

"Yes." Pamela flashed him an understanding smile. "The smallest one—" She pointed. "See there, the one with the single forward mast?"

He leaned close so his gaze could follow her finger. "I do."

"That's a cat boat. The majority of those are three-masted schooners. The largest of the schooners travels to England or the West Indies for trading. The ones with two masts are ketch rigs."

Her knowledge fascinated him, and he wondered if she'd have a hard time living away from the ocean. "You certainly know a lot about them."

"My family is in shipping." Pamela raised an eyebrow in obvious irony. "The problem with our business is storms, pirates, or other calamities...." She let out a slow breath. "Two of our ships sunk this year, taking down with them valuable cargoes.... But the deaths our crews...." Her shoulders sagged, and she shook her head. "A terrible loss. I knew some of the officers..."

At the sight of her sadness, he reached for her hand and squeezed.

Pamela briefly allowed him to comfort her before she pulled away her hand. "My father ensures that our sailors' families are compensated for life, no matter the financial burden to us. Most ship owners don't do so."

The Burke-Smythes are good people. He stared at the sea.

Regardless of the danger, an unexpected tug of longing pulled him toward the ocean. "Working outdoors with good men, fine horses, and healthy cattle is a blessing, yes indeed. But I'm mighty tempted to climb on board one of those ships and sail out to sea—explore the four corners of the earth." He stretched out the words into a drawl. "Which is really a strange sayin' considering the world is round—or so my schoolteacher led me to believe."

She laughed as he'd hoped. "This is only the bay. The ocean is even more vast."

"'Till my soul is full of longing, for the secret of the sea.'"

She joined him in quoting Longfellow's words. "'And the heart of the great ocean, sends a thrilling pulse through me.'"

"Bravo, Pamela. A perfect poem to express my sentiments."

Dipping a chin for a moment, she colored up. "Would you like to get out and have a closer look at the ships?"

"I would." John hesitated. "But the dock area might be too rough for a lady." He wouldn't want to put her in danger. "Perhaps I'll return another day. Right now, I'd rather find someplace quiet and peaceful." *More romantic.*

"How about we drive along the Charles River? The park area is quite lovely."

Although reluctant to leave the view of the sea, John took one last glance, imprinting details of the scene, and the warm feelings that were deepening toward his companion, and flicked the reins. The gray started into a steady walk.

Pamela directed him toward the river, where he reined in the horse under the shade of the trees and set the brake. Seeing the manicured park made him miss the untamed wilderness of Montana Territory.

He inhaled the smell of trees and grass combined with sea air and stared out at the water, which looked far more placid than the rivers he was familiar with. *This seems like a good place to propose.* He wondered if they should get out and stroll along the paths or remain in the surrey. *Perhaps remain.* He liked having her so close to him.

"Is being in the city hard for you?"

Keeping hold of the reins, he shifted to face her. "I'm used to wide open spaces. So many people live here, many of them elegant enough to make me stop and stare. Actually, I *did* stop and stare a time or two my first days in the city. In Montana Territory, I'm surrounded by simple, rustic folk—the salt of the earth—and not very many of them at that. The deer and the elk outnumber the humans." He grinned at her, enjoying her widening eyes. "And the grizzly bears outnumber the people."

Her mouth rounded into an O. "What about Indians?"

"We have them, if that's what you're asking." *Does the idea frightened her?*

"Yes."

"Nearest are the Blackfoot, Salish, and Crow tribes. None too close, though. Mostly, they're peaceable. Helped out my grandparents back in the day. From time to time, some will ride through my land, and I give them a haunch of beef. They're like most people—treat them right, and they'll treat you right."

She nodded in encouragement for him to go on.

"In Boston, there are so many *strangers*. Rare to meet a stranger in Sweetwater Springs. And a woman new to town is scarcer than hen's teeth. Her appearance is well nigh a cause for a celebration."

She laughed and fiddled with the ribbons of her bonnet. "Tell me more about Montana Territory.

"You get used to living in the wild. Making do. In the course of a day, the temperature can change from freezing cold to burning hot, so you'd better always be prepared for changeable weather."

John realized he sounded discouraging. *Hardly a way to sell Pamela on moving West.*

But I have to be honest about what she'll face.

Better add something positive. He pushed his hat back. "We have plenty of natural springs in our area. The cool springs have the sweetest water you'll ever taste—hence the name of our town.

And it's never too cold for a Montanan to sit in a natural hot spring, even if it means your wet hair turns into icicles."

Her hand rose to cover her mouth, and her eyes widened.

He laughed at her shocked expression.

Pamela lowered her hand. "Hot springs outdoors? In the winter?"

"Hot springs feel down right good to soak in anytime, especially when the air's cold outside. The hot water soothes sore muscles and is good for what ails you. But I also have a river through my property. I've dammed up a spot that makes for a nice swimming hole when it's hot in the summer."

A blush rose in her cheeks, and she glanced to the side.

"Very refreshing," he teased, just to watch the pink deepen.

"I've heard it's so cold there…long winters."

"Yes, but *I've heard*—" he echoed "—from some settlers who came from other states…that the cold often doesn't seem as bad as what they'd experienced where they come from because the air is very dry; it lacks humidity." He shrugged. "But I wouldn't know about that."

Pamela fanned her face with her hand. "You stick around here for the summer and you'll learn about humidity."

Her words sobered him. Not only wouldn't he stick around for several months, he couldn't stay for several more weeks. Hardly long enough to properly court a woman. *Will I lose the opportunity to wed Pamela because I can't give her the time she might need?* If she rejected him, he'd have to start all over on his wife hunt.

The thought of doing so almost nauseated him, and John knew right then and there that he didn't want another woman.

I've found my bride.

Pamela watched Mr. Carter's resolute expression, and she wondered what he was thinking. Having to invite her because

Elizabeth had been already engaged was really too bad. Her friend would have enjoyed this time with the rancher, especially learning more about his home. Pamela tucked away the details, storing up the information so she could impart all to her friend when next they were together.

But even as she thought of Elizabeth marrying Mr. Carter, at the same time, Pamela couldn't help the dreamy vision of bathing with him in a hot spring, touching each other as the snowflakes swirled around them. She let out a sigh. *So romantic.* Shivers coursed through her body.

The next minute, Pamela became aware of her thoughts. *No!* She wrenched her mind away from the image, ashamed of coveting a relationship with the man meant for her friend.

Mr. Carter shifted the reins into one hand and gave her an uncertain smile. With his free hand, he reached for hers, his thumb playing over her knuckles.

Even through her gloves, she could feel his touch—a delightful shock.

"Miss Burke-Smythe…I came to Boston in search of a wife. Someone with a good heart who could adapt to life on a Western ranch. I know it would be a lot for you to give up…but would you do me the honor of marrying me?"

The words buzzed in Pamela's ears. Her body tensed, and she stared at him in shock.

His eyes pleaded. "I know it's too soon. You should have a proper courtship where you have time to come to care for me as I do you. But if we wed, I'd be willing to delay…physical relations until you were comfortable with me."

After a traitorous thump of her heart, Pamela could think only of Elizabeth. Mr. Carter was supposed to give her friend a new life. *I can't tell her this. I don't want to hurt her.*

Mr. Carter must have decided to aim his sights lower than the beautiful, wealthy Miss Hamilton—settle on someone he could see had no hopes of marriage, a woman who'd jump at the chance to land a husband, any husband. Her stomach clenched against the pain of being second best. Her mouth dried, and she couldn't even find words to turn him down. All she could do was shake her head.

Sadness jumped into his eyes, so quickly masked that Pamela doubted she'd even seen the reaction. He released her hand and took back the reins.

The loss of connection was instant, but she couldn't allow herself to feel bereft.

"I'll take you home, then."

Pamela nodded, twisting her hands in her lap.

Perhaps now he'll allow himself to court Elizabeth. She'd have to tell her friend to give the rancher some stronger hints about her willingness to marry and move to the West. Surely, all Mr. Carter needed was some encouragement regarding the success of his suit. Then he'd propose, wed Elizabeth, and become the happiest of men.

Pamela wouldn't allow her heart to break at the thought.

Chapter Seven

Another ball, another social activity I want even less to attend than the previous one. Her heart heavy, footsteps dragging, Pamela moved through the Spencer family ballroom searching for Elizabeth. After she spoke to her friend, she'd resolved to linger just as long as was politely necessary before making her escape back to the comfort of her home.

Pamela spotted Elizabeth in animated discussion with Sylvia Jordan, who wore a pink satin and lace dress and sparkled with happiness from her recent betrothal. Elizabeth had donned a pale green silk gown that blended well with the gold velvet draperies framing the stained-glass window the two stood next to. Normally, Pamela would have joined their conversation. But today, she wasn't in the mood to talk—not even with her two closest friends.

Two elderly ladies passed by with gracious nods in her direction.

She forced a smile in return before easing to the side of the room, until she was in Elizabeth's line of sight. When Elizabeth saw her, Pamela made a discreet *come here* gesture.

Elizabeth's brow furrowed. She smiled at Sylvia and excused herself before hurrying over. "What's wrong?"

I can't tell you.

Pamela tried to dissemble. "What could possibly make you say such a thing?" she said in a light tone.

Elizabeth grabbed Pamela's hand, her expression grave. "I know you, Pam. So, it's no use trying to hide your feelings from me. Come." She pulled her behind a potted palm that screened them from curious eyes.

No one was in earshot, so Pamela decided to admit a sliver of the truth. "I'm sad at the thought of us parting. Boston and Montana Territory...." She shook her head. "So far apart."

"I know." Elizabeth squeezed her hand. "The only fly in the ointment of wedded bliss."

Pamela couldn't help but roll her eyes. "*That's* how you describe marriage?"

Her friend laughed. "That's how I describe marriage to *John Carter.*"

"Beth," Pamela said, feeling an urgent need to share her thoughts. "I have the feeling Mr. Carter is not aware of his own worth and is perhaps reluctant to propose. He needs stronger hints." Her cheeks burned at the truth she kept hidden—Mr. Carter's mistaken proposal to her.

Elizabeth stopped laughing and gave Pamela a searching look. "You couldn't hint to him?"

Grateful her friend understood, Pamela shook her head.

Elizabeth reached over and tucked strands of hair behind Pamela's ears. "Oh, Pam. Dear, dear Pam. I understand. Mr. Carter shall have his hints. I'll make sure of it."

Even though her insides felt hollow, Pamela forced herself to smile. "Good. Then all will be set to rights." She looked out on the dance floor, her gaze skimming the crowd for a familiar lanky figure. "There Mr. Carter is now. In the corner to the right. I'll leave you two..." She pulled her hand from Elizabeth's grasp and walked away as fast as she could without giving the appearance of fleeing, even if she most definitely was.

I can't bear to watch them together... See the moment when he learns the truth and realizes his heart's desire.

Her back to the dance floor, Pamela covered her cheeks with

her hands. She let out a strained breath before scurrying to an alcove to hide. *I just need a few minutes to compose myself.*

Later, I'll be calm…prepared. I'll be able to greet their announcement with the true joy they both deserve.

I won't give up. The potted palm didn't hide Pamela and Elizabeth from John. He saw Pamela searching the room for someone, only to stop when she saw him.

Hope leaped. His heart knocking against his chest, he started in their direction.

Perhaps I surprised her with my sudden declaration. Maybe she's still considering my offer, and I should press my suit.

But Pamela turned away without acknowledging him.

John halted, his stomach twisting as he watched her flee from him, taking with her his last vestiges of hope. She hadn't reconsidered his offer, after all.

He wanted to leave the ball, to crawl into a dark cave and lick his wounds. *Time to admit failure and go home.*

With a raised chin, draconian expression on her beautiful face, Elizabeth advanced on him. She looked about to breathe fire at his head for daring to ask Pamela to marry him and obviously upsetting her.

He braced himself. In politeness, there was no way of avoiding the woman, even if he wanted to.

"Mr. Carter, we are going to dance," Elizabeth said in clipped tones, giving him no time to object. She took his arm and tugged him toward the floor.

He cocked an eyebrow. "We are?" Even as he challenged her, John allowed her to pull him to an empty area where they assumed a ready position. A slow waltz started, and he had no trouble finding the pattern. *I have Pamela to thank for my newfound comfort with dancing.*

John didn't even attempt to swallow the sudden lump in his throat that robbed him of his ability to speak. Elizabeth might have dragged him out here, but he didn't have to talk to her. He'd let her speak her piece and be done with it.

For half a turn around the floor, she remained quiet. Then, as if coming to a decision, she raised her chin. "Mr. Carter, John, I will be blunt with you. I believe that you are courting my dear Pamela. Although I hate the thought of being forever separated from her, I believe you are a good man and would make her happy."

He choked, not believing what he'd heard. Evidently, Pamela hadn't brought her friend up to speed on the latest developments.

"As you've no doubt noticed, Pamela is shy and doesn't value her own worth. Your courtship will proceed more quickly if you are direct. Mere hints of your esteem will not be heard."

He almost stopped short. Only the need to avoid drawing attention and creating gossip kept his feet moving. "Elizabeth, this very afternoon, I asked Pamela to marry me." For the first time, he saw the woman shaken from her composure.

Her mouth gaped before she abruptly pressed her lips together. "That cannot be."

"I speak the truth."

Elizabeth waited while he guided them around a nearby couple. Once out of their hearing, she raised her brows. "You were direct with your proposal?"

"Does *Would you do me the honor of marrying me* sound clear enough to you?" John didn't bother to keep the edge of frustration out of his voice.

Frowning, she let out a long exhale. "I don't understand. It's clear to me she has feelings for you." Elizabeth remained silent for a few measures. "In fact, right before we started this dance, Pamela—" She broke off the sentence, and her forehead smoothed. "Why that *ninny!*" She let out a peal of laughter.

John waltzed them to the side of the room, where they could

unobtrusively leave the dance floor. He took her by the elbow and propelled her to the corner. "What are you talking about?"

"Pamela thinks you and I—" she gestured between the two of them "—are interested in *each other*. She's being noble in refusing you."

Her words knocked him off balance. "How could she believe that?"

"In the beginning, you did direct your attention toward me," she said with an accepting smile. "But when you wisely realized Pamela would make you a far superior wife, you focused on her. Mrs. Burton and I have been quietly aiding your efforts. Perhaps we've been too subtle. I hadn't realized she still thought you were interested in me." She shook her head in apparent disbelief. "Ninny," she repeated in a fond tone.

He listened to Elizabeth with rising hope.

"Pamela's very protective of me, John."

"Oh, course," he said with an impatient dip of their joined hands.

"Let me explain. You've heard about the deaths of my parents and fiancé?" She raised her brows in inquiry.

"I'm sorry for your loss."

"Pamela has worried about me these last two years. She provided the lifeline to which I clung when the dark waters of grief threatened to drown me. She has shed tears with me—not only those of empathy, but from her own grief—my parents were a second family to her. Richard…" Her voice broke… "A friend, who grew to be as dear as a brother to her. I know how much she longs for me to be well." Tears started into her eyes. "She was willing to sacrifice her happiness for mine." Her voice dropped to a whisper. "Such great love."

The description of Pamela's devotion endeared her to him even more. He whipped out his handkerchief and handed the material to her. "She's a remarkable woman."

Elizabeth dabbed her eyes. "I'm going to miss her so when she leaves with you."

"Pamela turned me down," John reminded her. But this time the memory didn't sting as much. To put her friend's happiness over her own would indeed be like the special woman he'd come to care for. "Let's go to her." Elizabeth pulled on his arm. "We will correct that mistake this instant."

Tucked in her alcove, trying not to cry, Pamela twisted her handkerchief first one direction, then the other. She'd taken out the cloth just in case her tears spilled over, but was determined not to need it.

From the corner of her eye, she glimpsed swift movement. She looked up to see Elizabeth and John—*no, I mustn't allow myself to think of him in such a familiar manner*—Mr. Carter bearing down on her. She inhaled with sharp dismay. Here came the news that would both thrill her and break her heart.

In her apparent eagerness, Elisabeth practically towed the rancher toward Pamela, her face alight.

It was obvious to Pamela that he'd proposed, and her friend had accepted. She tried to take a breath through the constriction in her lungs. *I'm not ready.* She plastered on a smile. *I will greet their news with a cheerful spirit. They will never know of my true feelings.*

"Pamela Marie Burke-Smythe! Dropping more hints, indeed."

At her friend's accusing tone, Pamela drew herself up. She waved toward where Elizabeth held Mr. Carter's arm. "Looks like my advice was useful."

Elizabeth rolled her eyes. "Oh, it was useful, all right. Although not in the way you intended."

What?

"We had a frank talk." Elizabeth glanced up at Mr. Carter. "I discovered John asked you to marry him."

Pamela gasped, her throat tightening.

"Why didn't you tell me?" Elizabeth shook her head and let go of John, holding up her hand to forestall whatever Pamela was going to say. "I want to be clear, Pam. I am not, nor have I been, interested in John Carter as a husband. I told you the truth when I said my darling Richard will hold my heart forever. I've only wanted John as a potential husband for my *best friend.*"

Pamela placed a hand on her chest, studying Elizabeth's face. *Is she telling the truth? Could she really pass up a man as fine as John Carter?*

Elizabeth took Pamela's hand and tugged down her arm, then she twined her fingers with Pamela's. "You will make the perfect rancher's wife, dearest. And become a maternal influence to that poor grief-stricken boy."

Pamela couldn't speak. She could only hug her friend. "Thank you for untangling this situation."

Elizabeth withdrew from the embrace. "Now. I believe John has an important question for you?" She gave him a flirty look and a flick of a wrist. "Go on, cowboy," she drawled.

They all burst into laughter, and Elizabeth moved away.

Overcome with joy, Pamela covered her mouth with her hand, staring up at John.

I don't care if I'm second choice! He's my John, and I will make him a good wife.

John stared after Elizabeth, an expression of admiration on his face. "Your friend is one fine woman, and I'll be forever grateful to her."

Doubt marred her happiness. Just because Elizabeth didn't want John didn't mean he wouldn't have chosen her if possible.

If that's the case, perhaps in time he will forget any attraction for Elizabeth and come to care for me.

"If she hadn't cornered me to discover my intentions, I'd have retreated brideless to Montana Territory with my tail tucked between my legs." His eyes warm, John extended his hand to her and waited, seemingly willing to remain in that posture all day until he coaxed a reaction from her.

Tentatively, she slipped her fingers into his. The warmth of his large hand, even through their gloves, heated hers and set her pulse racing.

"Pamela," he began.

Clearly, he was thinking that she'd already refused him. To save him the anxiety he must be feeling, with her free hand she covered his lips with her fingertips to stop him from repeating the question. "Yes, John, I'd be honored to become your wife."

With a smile of joy, he caught her hand and pressed a kiss to her palm. "What do you say…shall I take you home and talk to your father?"

Chapter Eight

After John's departure for Boston, Nick abandoned the ranch house and joined the cowboys, not liking to spend the evenings by himself. He'd claimed an empty bed in the corner of the bunkhouse, where he could be alone, yet still be part of the group.

The men mostly let him be—a contrast from before the accident, when they'd ruffled his hair and ribbed him every chance they'd had. And unlike John, they didn't expect him to talk. He could lie on his bed and listen while the men played cards or checkers, often swapping stories as old as the hills. Even Nick had heard them a time or two. But every once in a while, a new one livened up the evening.

Not that he much cared. Since the death of his family, his insides had frozen, even if his body mechanically went about the business of living.

After supper, the men started to speculate on Chuck Dodd's whereabouts. The ranch hand was late in returning from a trip to town. The speculations had varied from the likely—he stayed at the saloon too long—to the ridiculous—a wealthy female visitor had laid eyes on him, instantly fallen in love, and dragged him off to Preacher Norton.

But beneath the banter flowed an undercurrent of worry. Unsaid, but obviously on all the men's minds, was how the Sanders family had left for town and never returned.

As Nick speculated about the possibilities, he heard a thud outside on the narrow porch, followed by a jingle of spurs.

Chuck burst into the bunkhouse, his reddened blue eyes ablaze. He waved a telegram. "Boss done got himself a woman!" He climbed on the nearest bed as if onto a stage, squinted at the paper, and slowly read the words. "Arriving home on 10th with Mrs. Carter. Boxes and instructional letter shipped." He finished reading.

The rest of the men whooped. They slapped each other on the back, then passed the telegram around so each cowboy could peer at the words, even if he couldn't read them. Someone hunted up a calendar, and after a heated argument over today's date, they decided their boss would be home with his wife on Thursday.

Vey Garrett ran a hand through his shoulder-length hair. "We'd better look presentable. Although——" he glanced at the small shaving mirror over the washstand. "Some of us have more to *present* than others."

Nick looked over at the cowboy. The man was vain about his thick blond locks, and no amount of razzing from the other hands made him act any different.

"I 'spose we'll have to wash our faces and hands," grumbled old Frank, who had barely a tooth in his mouth.

"Yep," agreed Beans Brown, with a bob of his balding head. "Womenfolk set great store by cleanliness, that they do." He shook his head as if puzzled.

Nick figured baths for all the hands were in order. Or so his ma would have said. Thinking about her, he winced, the pain still as knife-sharp as when his family had died. Maybe worse. For a long time, he'd still believed they'd be coming home, even though he'd seen them dead and buried.

Dora Sanders wouldn't have been pleased that her son hadn't bathed every Saturday like clockwork, whether he needed it or not. *She'd be right ashamed of me. Grab me by my ear, haul me off to the hot spring, push me in, throw a bar of soap at me, and tell me to scrub up, or she'd be doing it for me.* He almost smiled at the vision.

Maybe I should clean up before the new missus gets here. But a wave of anger blocked out his half-formed thought of bathing before John's return. If his ma wanted him clean, then she should be here to make sure it happened. Irrational or not, he couldn't shake the feeling.

The mood in the bunkhouse, which had remained somber for the last six months, now became charged with excitement. The hands speculated about the type of woman John had married and if she was a good cook. When the betting started up on whether she'd be a blonde, brunette, or redhead, Nick slipped out the door, took a breath of the clean night air, and headed for the pasture and his rock.

His black-and-white dog, Bandit, lay waiting outside the bunkhouse, ears pricked.

Nick whistled.

She trotted over and thrust her nose into his hand, as happy to see him as if he'd been gone weeks instead of half an hour.

They fell into step, heading toward the horse pasture. Overhead, the three quarter moon cast barely enough light to see by. But his feet knew the way. Since Bandit was with him, Nick entered the gate and walked the long way to the rock. The horses were bunched on the far side, black shadows in the darkness.

He reached the shoulder-height boulder and climbed up. Scrambling to the top of the rock used to be an effort. Now his legs had grown long enough to hang over the sides. He settled in a comfortable spot, leaned back, and looked at the sky.

With a doggie sigh, Bandit settled down at the base to keep guard.

Nick had spent a lot of time on this rock lately, whenever chores allowed. He even came here when he couldn't sleep.

Tonight, he stared at the cold swath of blackness, the pinpricks of starlight. He liked to imagine the stars were windows to heaven and that Ma and Pa and Marcy stood on the other side and watched him. Each time he came to his rock, he chose different stars for them. Sometimes the three lights were grouped together, sometimes he picked isolated spots. On this night, he picked a bright one for his mother since she'd been on his mind. Pa had a star that reminded him of a sentinel, standing watchful near a clump. And Marcy was near Ma—a faint light that befitted her age.

Normally the ritual comforted him. But tonight, his thoughts drifted to John's new wife. Changes were in store, and Nick had learned to his deep regret that change meant he might end up hurtin' somehow.

Elizabeth came over early to help Pamela dress on her wedding day. After the maid, Jean, had styled Pamela's hair, they'd dismissed her so they could spend these last minutes alone. Elizabeth helped Pamela into her underskirt and carefully lifted the dress over her head.

"I'm glad we chose cream-colored silk," Elizabeth said, working the row of tiny buttons up the back. "I think the color is more becoming on you than white." She reached the final button at the top. "There." She turned Pamela to face the oval mirror standing in the corner and fluffed out the skirt.

Pamela looked at herself and caught her breath, amazed at the image she made.

The dress of silk faille was worn over an A-line crinoline and a pleated and ruffled silk underskirt. A wide flounce of handmade Brussels lace edged the bodice, the ends of the three-quarter sleeves, and the bottom of the basque. The sweeping train, which Pamela had insisted the dressmaker make removable, was lined with heavy ecru satin. Silk roses clustered above the train gave the illusion of a bustle.

Pearl drops hung from her earlobes, and her veil, draped back over her head for now, was anchored by a crown of faux pearls and crystals.

"Oh, Beth. This gown is beautiful!"

"*You* are beautiful, Pam. John's eyes will light up when he sees you."

Pamela glanced at her friend, resplendent in blue-green silk, and shook her head. Beautiful Elizabeth cast her into the shade. But as she studied herself in the mirror, Pamela realized today she didn't care. *John has chosen me to be his wife!* She, who'd been on her last hopes, was getting married to a man she adored.

She tried to inhale, but Elizabeth had tightly laced Pamela's corset, making her waist more slender than usual. She shifted sideways to admire her flat stomach. But the improvement in her figure came at a stiff price. She could barely breathe and hoped she wouldn't faint dead away during the ceremony.

Elizabeth took a small cloth-wrapped parcel from her reticule and placed it in Pamela's hand. "Something borrowed." Lifting a hand, she touched Pamela's earrings. "You already are wearing your mother's pearls. This is something both new and blue."

"There was so much to think about this week, I didn't even consider what I'd need for good luck."

"Well," Elizabeth drawled. "I did have *slightly* less to do than you did." She unfolded the cloth to expose a blue glass ring chatelaine in the shape of a heart with a raised gold and enamel pattern.

"Oh, Beth, thank you! It's beautiful." Pamela lifted the chatelaine, designed to be discreetly carried, unscrewed the top, and sniffed. *Orange blossom.* "This smells heavenly." She dabbed the scent on her wrists and neck, then carefully closed the container and slid the ring over the middle finger of her right hand. The tiny bottle fit perfectly in her palm.

Pamela fingered the lace and embroidered handkerchief that had surrounded the chatelaine. "I recognize this." She touched the monogram in the corner. "Your mother's."

Sudden tears gleamed in Elizabeth's eyes, and she bit her lip.

Pamela missed her own mother with a sharp stab of longing. She took her friend's hand. "We mustn't cry. It wouldn't do to have both of us walk up the aisle with red eyes." Her mother had died when she was ten, so she'd had more years than Elizabeth to become used to her maternal absence. *But not today.*

"Our mothers would have been so happy, Pam. They would have been here clucking away at you, making sure everything is perfect."

Pamela sent Elizabeth a loving look. "Well, I have *you* for that."

The sentence hung in the air. Neither commented that Pamela was leaving tomorrow for Montana Territory with her new husband.

Elizabeth glanced at the small clock on the dressing table. "We're finished fifteen minutes early. Let me help you sit. We don't want you to wrinkle." She pulled the train backward so Pamela could perch on the edge of her four-poster bed.

"You're still too pale, though." Elizabeth leaned over and pinched Pamela's cheeks. "That's better. We must remember to do that again before you walk up the aisle."

The two friends stared at each other as if forming a memory.

Elizabeth was the first to break the silence. "I can't believe this is it. You're actually getting married!"

"The reality is just now hitting me. I've been so busy all week, I can't believe I'm sitting here with nothing to do. Too bad I can't breathe."

Elizabeth chuckled.

An echoing laugh tried to bubble up inside Pamela but became trapped by the tightness of her corset. Wincing, she held up her hand in protest. "Don't get me started, Beth. I'll probably collapse from lack of air."

Her eyes dancing, Elizabeth shook her head. "You should have been wearing your corset strings tied tighter all along. Then you'd be used to the feeling by now."

"It didn't matter before."

"Well, soon it won't again. I doubt you'll want a tight corset on a ranch."

"That will be a relief." She paused, sighed. "My mind keeps going in circles. I keep thinking I've forgotten something."

"Silly," Elizabeth scoffed in a loving voice. "Just write me if you need anything, and I'll send it out to you."

With a sigh, Pamela tilted her head to the side until her temple rested on the bedpost. She was careful not to disturb her hair, which had more than twice the amount of pins she usually wore to keep her coiffure in place so no strands slipped loose. She needed these few minutes to relax and compose herself.

The week before the wedding had passed in a flurry of activity as Pamela prepared for the ceremony and the reception, and did some necessary shopping—not only for her trousseau, but also for household items she thought she'd need. Her preparations kept her too busy and tired to dwell on the fact that she was about to leave all she knew and loved. She knew the feelings would hit her but suspected she'd have plenty of time in the future to miss what and whom she'd left behind.

In addition, Pamela had waves of callers wanting to gossip about her future husband and her upcoming wedding. Seemed half her female acquaintances were awed by her intention to move to Montana Territory, and the rest thrived on relaying every bit of bad news—often involving bloody skirmishes with Indians—they'd heard, read, or imagined about life in the West. Although Pamela had little time with her fiancé, who was busy with his own concerns, she was grateful he called upon her each day. His visits helped reassure her.

John enjoyed hearing her repeat the tales she'd heard, sometimes slapping his leg and roaring with laughter, which did more to assuage her fears than any words could. Sometimes he'd catch her up in a spontaneous hug that warmed her to her toes. Once he'd made a comment about what a gift it was to laugh.

He also explained the reality behind the gossip, as when Mrs. Albrecht had said their two-story ranch house would be buried in snow to the roof—as if Boston winters couldn't be bitterly cold. John assured her that after a series of storms, snow up to the first floor windows was more the usual limit. His ranch hands knew to clear the snow between the house, outbuildings, and the barn at the earliest opportunity.

In a whirlwind of shopping, she'd purchased enough supplies to stock a pantry and cellar for the next five years. She and Elizabeth had selected china in a rose pattern and shipped the eighteen place settings and matching serving pieces, as well as silverware, to Sweetwater Springs. John had never even seen the service, telling her to choose what she liked. Then he'd gone out and bought a china cabinet for her to display them and shipped it too.

Pamela had augmented the contents of her hope chest, buying down featherbeds and pillows, linens, towels, and brown velvet curtains, along with lace panels that she could cut to fit the windows.

Her fiancé had offered to pay for her purchases, but Pamela's father had put his foot down, declaring their business setbacks didn't mean they were in such dire straights that he couldn't properly outfit his daughter, buy what she needed to start her new life, give her a beautiful wedding, and send her off with a little money, even if the sum wasn't the dowry that he'd previously planned for her.

In between shopping and socializing, Pamela had spent time with the housekeeper and cook, writing down the advice of both ladies, and taking lessons so she could make meals for her husband and Nick. When she was small, she'd been indulged by the cook who had encouraged her love of baking, teaching her how to make cookies and cakes. This week's attempts at baking bread had been a disaster with the loaves turning out dry and lumpy. Hopefully she'd learned enough from her mistakes to not repeat them. But she still had her doubts.

Elizabeth glanced at the clock and then touched Pamela's gloved hand. "It's time, dearest." She pressed her lips together to hold back emotion and walked toward the door. "I'll go tell your father you're coming down."

Pamela waited until the sound of Elizabeth's footsteps had

died away before she stood. With a sad lump in her throat, she glanced around her girlhood room. The space was denuded of her familiar possessions, which were already packed for the journey, except for what she'd need for today and tomorrow. Some of her old dresses and her battered gardening hat still hung in the wardrobe for her maid to take or put into the poor box.

When next Pamela entered her bedroom, she'd be a wife and would never again sleep in the narrow four-poster bed. Tonight, she and John were staying in the guest room. Tomorrow, they would set out for the train station.

Just the thought of sharing a bed with John made her heart flutter. Suddenly anxious to be married, Pamela picked up her skirts and hurried out the door.

At the top of the staircase, she paused and looked down into the entryway to see her family and Elizabeth waiting for her. Her father and three brothers stared up at her with an expression of shock and pride on their faces, and her two small nieces, standing with their mother, bounced in excitement.

Pamela took each stair slowly, realizing what must appear to be a stately descent was really just her attempt to discreetly catch her breath with each step.

At the bottom of the stairs, her father held out his hand.

Pamela slipped her gloved fingers into his.

"You look beautiful, my daughter." Sudden tears gleamed in his eyes. "I wish your mother could be here." He leaned close and kissed her cheek.

Pamela inhaled the familiar scent of bay leaf soap and clung to him for a moment. "She is, Papa. She wouldn't let me get married without her presence."

"Our baby girl, all grown up." He set her back, sending a teasing glance to her older brothers. "We'd begun to think all we'd have were boys."

Unspoken for a moment, the memory of little Mary shimmered between them. *She's here, too. I can almost see her holding hands with Mama.*

Her oldest brother Ronald, tall and blond, looked like their mother with his narrow face and blue eyes. "Well, with my two little daughters, the female score is now equal. Although that might change in a year or two when you start popping out babies."

Frowning, his wife poked an elbow into his ribs.

Ronald raised his eyebrows, mouthing innocently, *what?* He leaned forward to kiss Pamela's cheek. "You do look rather dazzling for a little sister."

Babies. The very word dazed her. Just a short time ago, Pamela had thought she was fated to be a maiden aunt.

She accepted kisses from her sister-in-law and two other brothers and allowed them to escort her to the carriage. Because her gown and long train took up so much space, she and her father rode alone to the church. Still struck by the knowledge that by this time next year she might be a mother, Pamela sat quietly with her hand resting in her father's.

The coach pulled up to Christ the Shepherd Cathedral. Her father helped her out, while her family and Elizabeth spilled out of the other carriages. Sylvia Jordan, her other bridesmaid, must have been on the watch for them because she came hurrying out of the church and took charge of the train so it wouldn't touch the stone steps. She wore a matching dress to Elizabeth's figure-hugging blue-green.

The group climbed the steps to the cathedral, moving from the bright spring sunshine into the cool dimness of the church. Organ music played Handel's "Water Music," a selection Pamela had chosen.

Sylvia and Elizabeth led her to the ladies' retiring room. Outside the door, her father kissed her cheek again and said he'd wait in the vestibule. Inside, the music was muffled but still audible. Their bouquets, made of hot house white roses and orange blossoms, rested on a nearby table, perfuming the air.

Sylvia picked up the bigger bouquet, satin ribbons wound

around the stems, and handed the flowers to Pamela. "Such a special day, dear Pamela." She gave a pretend pout. "You're going away, you wretch. I can't believe you won't be here for my wedding." Her light tone covered up genuine sadness.

Pamela blinked back tears. "Don't get me started," she ordered. "Bad enough that Elizabeth already tried." She smiled at her friends, clinging to the last moments of intimacy with the three of them together, but also eager to be wed and start her new life.

The music changed to a piece by Brahms. The time for the ceremony drew near.

Elizabeth tucked the flowers tighter into Sylvia's dark blond chignon.

A knock sounded on the door.

Being closest, Elizabeth opened it.

Her father waited on the other side. "Are you ready?"

Pamela walked from the room. Once outside the inner doors, Elizabeth and Sylvia spread out her train, fussing to make sure the lace edges remained flat. The music flowed into a piece by Bach.

Halfway through the piece, Elizabeth leaned over and pinched Pamela's cheeks. "Beautiful, dear Pam."

With quick smiles, her bridesmaids pushed through the doors and left her to walk up the aisle.

She and her father stepped inside the sanctuary and halted by the first pew. The organ and trumpet swelled to "The Prince of Denmark's March."

Goosebumps cascaded over Pamela's skin, and champagne bubbles danced in her stomach.

Everyone rose with a hushed rustling. Their gazes played over her gown, her hair, her face, and reflected back admiration—an uncommon occurrence that she relished with deep appreciation.

And then Pamela saw her future husband, tall and handsome in a black suit. Before now, she'd thought she'd be nervous with everyone watching her, but Pamela only had eyes for her groom, and he for her. The rest of the room blurred into unimportance.

With a stately glide, she and her father moved up the aisle. Seeing the intensity in John's eyes, his happy smile, made her steps falter as her heart filled with hope.

Dear Lord, please may this marriage turn into a love match!

Before this last month, John had never considered his wedding beyond assuming he'd have one someday. Somehow, the years—too filled with ranch duties—had slipped by without him marrying. A good thing, for then he would have settled on someone other than Pamela Burke-Smythe, and he couldn't imagine any other lady but her at his side for life.

But if he *had* thought about his wedding, John would have assumed he'd marry in the church in Sweetwater Springs, with Reverend Norton conducting the ceremony and his friends lining the pews.

The reality could not be more different.

He waited for his bride in front of an ornately carved altar in a cathedral that was six times bigger and three times higher than the church at home. The box pews were filled with people he didn't know at all, with only a handful who were mere acquaintances sitting on the groom's side of the aisle.

Organ music changed from "Andante from Symphony I" by Johannes Brahms—not that he would have known the piece without Pamela and Reverend Wallis going over the order of the service with him—to 'Jesu, Joy of Man's Desiring,' which Mrs. Norton always played on the piano at the Christmas Eve service. The piece sounded far more impressive coming from the huge pipe organ.

Even with Ronald and James Burke-Smythe at his side in what should have been Andrew's role as best man, and Great-Aunt Hester sitting in the first row with her daughters, granddaughters, and their spouses, John felt alone. No individual was present in this cavernous room that he'd known more than three weeks.

As a trumpet joined the organ in Jeremiah Clark's triumphant march, John was glad Pamela had chosen the piece over the more traditional "Bridal Chorus" from Lohengrin. Even though he had familiarity with the music because Mrs. Norton had played the piece by Wagner at every wedding he'd attended.

The music sent goosebumps down John's arms, bringing him into stark awareness of the sanctity of this ceremony, the weight of the commitment he was about to make, the new life journey he and Pamela were about to embark on...together. Goosebumps shivered over his skin, and his legs trembled. He didn't chide himself for the unmanly reactions, just took some deep breaths to steady himself.

The bridesmaids appeared, first Sylvia, then Elizabeth. Pamela had selected only two handmaidens to attend her. The young women walked up the aisle, beautiful in bluish-green gowns. But then Pamela appeared in the open doorway on the arm of her father.

As he watched them move up the aisle toward him, John looked past the two ladies. He had eyes for no one but his bride. The delicate lace of her veil didn't hide her shining brown eyes and tremulous smile. *She walks in beauty...* The lines of Byron's poem floated through his mind.

Love, rich and warm, filled him, and John eagerly reached for her hand, drawing her close. His gaze never left her face, nor hers his. Her father stepped away.

Reverend Wallis beamed at them. "Dearly beloved. We are gathered here in the sight of God to unite this man and woman in holy matrimony."

In hushed voices, the two of them spoke their vows before God. John slipped a diamond ring on Pamela's finger and heard the minster pronounced them man and wife. He placed a tender kiss on his bride's lips—*the first of many*, he silently promised her.

Carried down the aisle by the triumphant strains of Mendelssohn's "Wedding March," the new Mr. and Mrs. Carter walked into the sunshine, ready to begin their new life.

Chapter Nine

After the wedding festivities, hand-in-hand, John escorted Pamela to the guestroom. He brought her fingers to his lips, sending a shiver down her spine, then excused himself so she would have privacy to change.

Instead of the regular oil lamps, long tapers on the dressing table and next to the bed cast a romantic glow around the room, and a fire burned in the fireplace. A vase of white roses perfumed the air. With a nervous shiver, Pamela glanced at the big bed with the elaborately carved headboard.

Her maid, Jean, rustled forward. "Congratulations on your marriage, madam."

"Thank you." She smiled at her maid. "And you too, Jean, on your approaching nuptials."

Pamela had asked Jean to move to Montana Territory with her, but the maid had chosen to remain and marry her childhood sweetheart instead. She hadn't had time to find a new maid—one who could also do household tasks—so Elizabeth had taken on the job of finding one and sending her West.

Jean removed the tiara and veil, then helped her out of the wedding gown. As lovely as the dress was, Pamela was glad to be free of the weighty material. Forty pounds of fabric and reinforcing garments was far too much to wear for hours.

As soon as the corset was unlaced, Pamela inhaled the first

full breath she'd had all day, then frowned at the deep gouges in the flesh of her waist and sides from the stays.

She rubbed the grooves to no avail, before shrugging. John had promised to wait for intimacy, and while she was eager for his embraces, she wasn't quite ready for complete surrender. Her husband wouldn't see the marks tonight, and in the future, she wouldn't wear her corset so tight.

Jean slipped Pamela's silk nightgown over her head, the material lighter than air, then helped her into a matching robe. She gestured for Pamela to sit in front of the dressing table and began to remove the hairpins from her heavy coif.

A soft knock sounded at the door.

At the sound, Pamela's heart thudded. "Come in." She turned toward the door.

John entered, looking as resplendent as a Mandarin prince in a black silk dressing gown embroidered with red Chinese symbols.

The sight drove away her nervousness. She raised her eyebrows.

He pulled a comical expression. "A present from Great-aunt Hester."

Pamela giggled. "You look quite splendid." She turned to her maid and smiled. "I can finish my hair. Thank you, Jean."

"Yes, madam." The maid bobbed a curtsey before leaving.

Pamela stared after her. "How strange to be called madam, not miss." She pulled a hair pin out of the braided and curled mass.

John walked over to stand behind her chair. "Good strange?" Watching her in the mirror, he placed his hands on her shoulders and began to knead the muscles.

"Mmm, very good strange."

He hit the tight spots and pressed.

She winced.

John immediately lifted his hands.

"No, no, don't stop. It feels wonderful. I just didn't realize how sore I was."

He resumed his massage of her shoulders and neck, his eyes on hers in the mirror.

Even through the delicate fabric, she could feel the callouses on his hands from rough outdoor work. He'd told her so many stories, and she took pleasure in the image of him riding the range, lifting a stray calf, joining the men in the spring branding. Under his ministrations, she began to relax. As her muscles loosened, Pamela became aware of a headache, caused by the heavy mass of hair anchored by dozens of pins. She reached up and pulled out one.

"Allow me to get the rest." He felt for each pin, making the slow removal of every one a sensual gesture instead of an ordinary task.

Her hair spilled over her shoulders and down her back. "What a relief. Half a dozen of those pins were stabbing my scalp all day."

He reached up and gently rubbed her head.

The pressure of his fingers felt so marvelous that a moan of pleasure escaped her lips.

"Why wear them then?" His brow wrinkled.

"I usually don't need so many. But I wanted my hair to be perfect, not have wild tendrils falling down."

He leaned over and dropped a kiss on the top of her head, fingered a loose strand near her ear. "I like your wild tendrils, and I don't want my wife to have a sore head. In fact, I won't mind if at home you just wear a braid down your back."

Pamela was about to protest the idea, but his fingers dug deeper into her scalp. The resulting pressure felt so blissful that all objections left her mind. She gave herself over to the pleasure of his touch.

After John thoroughly massaged her head, he reached over and picked up her brush from the dressing table. In silence, he began to stroke the brush through her hair, gently tugging through any tangles.

Pamela was mesmerized by the motion, so much more sensual than Jean's practical strokes. Pleasure bubbled inside, and she wanted to purr like a cat.

When he finished the first section, he ran his palm down the wavy fall. "Like silk," he murmured, then resumed brushing. "One hundred." John set the brush down on the dressing table, then blew out the candles.

The room darkened, lit only by the bedside candle and the orange coals in the fireplace. For a moment, they stared at each other in the mirror, their features shadowed, allowing the energy of a connection to thrum between them.

Taking her hand, John pulled her to her feet. He slid the robe off her shoulders and dropped it over the chair. "Into bed with you, dearest."

Feeling vulnerable, Pamela hastened to climb under the bedcovers.

John blew out the final candle. The room was plunged into darkness with only the coals glowing in the fireplace.

She heard the slither of his robe falling, but kept her gaze turned away. When John climbed into bed, she was relieved to feel the material of a night shirt brush her hand.

"Come here, wife." He gathered her to him, until she lay tucked against his side, her head resting on his shoulder. "Comfortable?"

"Oh, yes." She inhaled the man scent of him—her John—and entirely liked the strangeness of their embrace, her soft body cushioned next to his muscled one.

"Good," he murmured. "Relax now. We have plenty of time to know each other—the rest of our lives. Tonight is only the beginning."

Reassured by his words, Pamela snuggled closer. Greatly daring, she slipped her hand over his stomach.

He lightly ran his fingers up her arm.

Goosebumps feathered over her skin, and her breath hitched. He continued to stroke her with his fingertips, up and down her arms, sometimes straying down her back, or up to her face, across her cheeks and over her forehead.

Never had she felt such touches. She sighed with pleasure and tilted her face to his.

John rolled to his side, shifting her body to face him.

She tilted up her face, expecting a kiss.

His mouth descended, only to hover a hair's breath away from her lips.

She could have moved to meet him, but she didn't, enjoying the feel of his breath on hers, the anticipation of the press of their lips together, of being so intimately close.

After a long moment of stillness and silent connection, his lips brushed hers in the faintest of butterfly kisses.

Pamela felt the winged fluttering course over her skin and deep into her core.

With a slow slide of his fingers, he traced the curve of her cheek.

She pressed a kiss into his palm.

He ran his hand down her arm, then once again rolled onto his back, bringing her next to him.

Pamela lay with her cheek pressed against his chest, heard the slow beat of his heart. Love for this man—her dear husband— filled her, and she sent up a little prayer of thankfulness to God for bringing them together.

Soon, John's breathing deepened, and his muscles slackened.

She pressed a kiss to his chest, grateful for his care of her. After a few drowsy moments, Pamela followed her husband into sleep.

When Pamela awoke after a surprisingly sound rest, she was alone in the bed. But the dent in the pillow next to hers made her lips curl into a sensual smile, and she relived the cuddling with her husband. She stretched out her hand, admiring the sparkle of her diamond wedding ring, then pulled John's pillow to her nose, inhaling his now-familiar scent. The crackle of paper made her reach to find a note.

My dearest Pamela,

This morning when I awoke, you were asleep, and I didn't have the heart to wake you. Our journey to your new home begins today, and I hope you are as excited to get started as I am.

Your husband,

John

After admiring his bold scrawl, Pamela pressed the note to her chest. *My first love letter. I'll save it forever.*

She threw back the covers and rang for her maid, then donned her robe and hurried down the hall to the bathroom.

When she returned, Jean was in the room arranging a tray of tea and toast with a poached egg—Pamela's usual morning breakfast.

"Morning, Jean," Pamela practically sang the words.

"Morning, Miss Pamela, eh, I mean, Mrs. Carter."

Pamela smiled at the maid. "My new name takes some getting used to. I think with most brides, they have a long enough engagement to prepare themselves. I went from Miss Pamela Burke-Smythe to Mrs. John Carter in a week! And now, I have to ready myself to leave soon."

While Pamela ate, she listened as Jean gave her a running commentary on the last of the preparations, including the packing of her wedding gown into one of the trunks.

Pamela finished and washed her hands. Then Jean helped her dress in a garnet traveling outfit.

She and Elizabeth had chosen the traveling dress with narrow black-and-gold stripes running through the material and a small bustle behind. They'd allowed for an additional two inches of material in the waist so Pamela wouldn't have to wear her corset too tightly laced. The dark fabric wouldn't show any dirt encountered during the trip.

Feeling almost pretty in the vibrant color, with the pink of excitement flushing her cheeks, Pamela set her new bonnet on her head and tied the garnet ribbons at a jaunty angle under her chin. She pulled on her gloves and slid the strings of her reticule over her wrist. Then she picked up her matching coat and draped the garment over her arm.

Jean left the room and soon returned, carrying a covered basket. Smoky was inside, nestled into a soft blanket.

The kitten let out a meow in protest.

"It will be okay, baby." Pamela had been keeping the basket in her room so the kitten could become familiar with it. But Smoky obviously didn't like being closed in and carried. Hopefully, he'd soon settle down. She was bringing along a shallow box and a bag of sand for the kitten to use along the way.

With one last approving look in the mirror, Pamela hurried out the door.

John waited impatiently in the entry for his bride with the four Burke-Smythe men—father and brothers—all ranged around him, eyeing him with expressions that told him as clearly as words, *You'd better take good care of Pamela.*

Since he'd already vowed before God to love and cherish his bride, John had no idea what else he could do to ease their minds. But he figured another promise might not go amiss. "I will do my best to keep my wife safe and happy."

Newton Burke-Smythe, a graying masculine version of his daughter, dropped a hand on John's shoulder. "I know that, son, else I wouldn't have let you marry her. But my only daughter will be far away from us, and we'll miss her."

"I hope you'll visit."

With a quick nod, Ronald grinned at him. "If I can talk the wife into it."

"We'd like that." His new sister-in-law had made her goodbyes the night before.

Before any of them answered, footsteps on the stairs had them all glancing up to see Pamela, looking as fashionable as if she was going for a stroll around the city, walking down the steps, carrying a coat and a square covered basket. Her eyes sparkled, and she glowed with happiness.

At the sight of her good spirits, her father and brothers relaxed their stiff postures.

John couldn't help a feeling of smugness.

Newton stepped forward. "I don't need ask if you are well. The pink in your cheeks right here—" he kissed her continental style "—tells me all I need to know."

Pamela's color deepened, and she dipped her chin.

Her brothers laughed.

A mew from the basket made John's good feelings flee. He had to repress a shake of his head. His wife's determination to bring her kitten on their journey had caused their only premarital spat, if the mild disagreement could even be called that. Not that he didn't want her to have a kitten. Goodness knows the barn could always use a cat to keep down the rodents, not to mention the occasional mouse that got into the house.

But he knew traveling would be difficult enough without having to see to the needs of a kitten. He'd offered to buy her one in Sweetwater Springs. But when she'd challenged him, John realized he didn't know where he'd actually obtain one. Not to mention that he couldn't resist her pleading expression.

Pamela shot a smile at John.

I didn't warn her how dirty this trip would be. I assumed she'd know to dress appropriately. Gripping the brim of his hat tighter, John hoped the upward turn of his lips hid his dismay.

In that moment, he became aware of a canyon between himself and his bride. In spite of the stories he'd told her, he hadn't prepared her enough, and his wife really had no idea of the kind of life she'd be living in Montana Territory. With a sense of shock, John realized he'd have to try to think ahead for what she'd require. Would he figure out when he needed to warn or guide her? Or would there be times when she couldn't possibly know something important that he took for granted?

Fear tightened his belly, and the weight of her dependency settled around his shoulders. *What if I fail?* He'd failed to protect his sister when some thinking on his part would have prevented the horrific accident that caused her death. In a few seconds, dozens of ways his bride could be hurt or killed raced through his mind. Pamela seemed to be a sensible woman, but Boston-sensible and Montana-sensible were two different things.

John clenched his jaw. He'd given a lot of thought to providing for a wife, but he'd never realized that her very life might be in his hands. "Pamela, you need to go change clothes." His concern made the words sound harsh. "The trip will take four days. We'll be sleeping on the train. There's no way you can possibly be comfortable in that contraption." He waved at her bustle.

Pamela frowned and glanced behind her as if she had no idea of what he meant. "It's only a small one. Practical."

She has no idea about practical.

"Trust me. You won't want a bustle, my dear. We'll be sleeping in our seats as best we can." He gestured to her dress. "And the smoke and cinders will ruin whatever you wear."

Her brother Ronald gave her a compassionate smile. "Though you look a delight in that."

Her father stepped forward. "Your husband is correct, my dear." He patted her shoulder. "I remember your mother's complaints when we took that train trip to New York. Montana Territory is a much longer journey."

Her face paled.

John motioned to the stairs. "Go change into something old and comfortable. Something you won't mind throwing away later."

His wife ran a hand over her skirt, then glanced at him, eyes wide, brows pulled together. "But everyone will be at the station to see us off." She flushed, a stricken look in her eyes. "I sound vain and silly, don't I?"

This time John's smile was genuine. "You sound like a new bride who wants to show off her trousseau. Too bad everyone won't see how pretty you look in that gown. But you'll dazzle the inhabitants of Sweetwater Springs later."

Her expression changed from distress to pleasure. "Very well. I'll put on one of my old dresses. I'd left them behind to go into the poor box."

John directed a pointed look at the coat she carried. "Do you have an old one, as well?"

"You have that ratty thing you garden in when the weather's cold," Ronald teased.

She wrinkled her nose at her brother before turning to John. "I suppose I'll need a different bonnet, too."

"That's quite a charming confection you're wearing," John said, softening his words with another smile. "But unless you want your new hat ruined…"

Pamela let out a long sigh. "Good thing I love to work in the garden. I have an ancient straw hat for that as well."

John tilted his head in curiosity. "Did you not expect me to have a garden?"

"Oh, no," she assured him with a slight wave of her hand. "I'm sure you do. I've purchased all new work clothes."

The men laughed.

John held in a smile, delighted with his wife's sweet naiveté, while still worried about her ability to quickly adapt to the West. "Go change, my dear," he said gently. "We don't want to miss the train."

Chapter Ten

John woke Pamela from dozing against his shoulder. "My dear, we're almost at Sweetwater Springs."

At his words, she startled, sat up, and smothered a yawn. "Oh, my." Glancing out the windows at the passing scenery, Pamela rolled her neck and shoulders, trying to work out the stiffness. Nervous anticipation pinched her stomach. She sniffed, disliking the acrid smell of smoke that clung to them.

John ran a hand over the kitten, sleeping on his lap. "Better put him back in the basket."

Smoky stretched all four legs.

Luckily, the kitten had adapted to their mode of travel, spending hours on Pamela's lap. He used the sandbox Pamela had brought along but had been off his feed. Hopefully, his appetite would return when they were settled. Yesterday, he'd decided to accept John as his human and had gifted him with lap time as well.

A wise choice. Throughout the interminable journey, her husband had remained patient with both her and Smoky, doing his best to ease her discomfort and entertain her with stories of the ranch. She felt as if she knew all nine cowboys and Nick, as well as his parents and grandparents—her future children's ancestors. He'd even told tales of his foreman and close friend, Andrew, smiling through many of them, although sometimes a shadow of pain darkened his eyes. If Pamela hadn't already fallen in love with her caring husband, she would have done so on this trip.

He brushed a few wayward strands of hair off her face. "Tired?"

"Fatigued by the journey, yes. I can't wait to get *home*." Pamela treasured the word. "But the nap did me good."

"I can't wait to get you home," John echoed with a teasing smile. Then his expression sobered. "I only hope you aren't disappointed."

This wasn't the first time he'd expressed such sentiments. Pamela let out a huffing breath. "And what if I am, John? Do you think me such a poor creature that I'll go into a decline? Lay around on a sofa and weep all day?"

"No, my dear." He shook his head, a ghost of a smile playing about his lips. "Never that."

"I'm not a woman who's discontented by nature. I can make the best of things. And we can make improvements, can we not?"

The worried look in John's eyes cleared. "Well," he drawled. "I put my foot down at the notion of improving the ranch house to match your Pa's."

She wrinkled her nose. "Silly man."

"You can spruce up the house to your heart's content. The place always seemed pretty big to me. I just rattled around. Mostly lived in the kitchen and slept in a bedroom. Then lately it's been Nick and me. But having seen that monstrosity you lived in…" An eyebrow arched as he met her gaze.

"Monstrosity." She laughed. "You're lucky I wasn't a Sofit daughter."

"A mansion for titans. The Sofit offspring must stand fifteen feet tall."

She thumped his leg with her knuckles.

Smoky stirred, opening sleepy eyes, then fell back asleep.

"You met Sophie Sofit, and she is my height."

He winked. "Only two young ladies made a memorable impression on me that night, and neither was Sophie Sofit."

Two ladies. She had a quick feeling of insecurity, easily pushed aside.

"As you know, my home is no Sofit mansion…but we can always add on." His tone sobered. "I do have something to confess, though."

Her shoulders tensed.

"I never moved out of my boyhood room."

Pamela looked askance at him.

"Never seemed right to sleep in my parents' bed."

Her body relaxed, and she nodded, understanding such sentiments.

"Then, when it probably would have been fine, the habit was already there, and I never thought to move." He shrugged. "Fact is, one room or another didn't change anything. I was only in there to sleep."

Thinking over this revelation, she pursed her lips. "You're all right with moving now?"

He grinned. "I think having you in my bed will make all the difference in the world."

Pamela remembered their wedding night in Boston and felt the heat of a blush rising in her face. Abruptly, she leaned over the empty seat in front of them to pick up her hat. With only a few people in the car, she and John had spread out their possessions. Her straw hat was now even more battered than when they'd set out—definitely fodder for the fire as soon as she was at the house and clean. She placed it on her head, then lifted the cat's basket over the seatback.

"Let me get him." John gently scooped up the kitten, who dangled boneless in his big hands. With care, he lowered him into the basket.

Smoky mewed in protest.

Pamela left the lid off, petting Smoky until he plopped down and curled into a ball. "There you go, baby." She peered out the window to the grasslands and the mountains beyond. "How much farther?"

"Just a few minutes. Keep watching. You'll see the first house right about...*now.*" He pointed to a shack that flashed by.

People live there? she thought in dismay. *If that's John's idea of a house...The big home I'm expecting might not be so nice after all.*

The train chugged past a sturdy log cabin, then started to slow at a cluster of buildings before jerking and shuddering to a stop, with a whoosh of brakes and steam.

A quick look at the more substantial structures allowed her to relax a bit.

John leaned over to drop a kiss on her lips. "Welcome to Sweetwater Springs, Mrs. Carter."

Although embarrassed the other passengers might have seen, Pamela couldn't help enjoying the sweetness of her husband's welcome. Given the public nature of their journey, since leaving Boston all they'd done was hold hands.

I'll never see these people again, she told herself. *It hardly matters what they think about John kissing me. What matters is my marriage!*

"A lovely welcome, my husband. Thank you."

John placed his hat on his head, stood, and reached for the basket. He shifted the handle into his other hand so he could help Pamela to her feet. He returned the basket to her and picked up their carpetbag before heading down the aisle, glancing back once to make sure she was following.

The conductor poked his head into their car. When he saw they were leaving, he smiled and nodded.

John walked down the steps first, then guided Pamela to the platform.

I've landed in Montana Territory! The unpainted wood of the depot looked raw, and she remembered John telling her the train had only recently come to this area.

Farther down the line, porters offloaded their trunks and various crates onto the platform.

She was relieved not to see anyone around—to have to make conversation with strangers was hard enough for her when she was looking her best. But to do so when she was grubby...

John released her hand, strode over to the men, reaching in his pocket to tip them some money.

Pamela followed at a slower pace. She stopped to look more closely at the town and couldn't help a pang of disappointment at the sight of the single road lined with false-fronted wooden structures. Unlike some of the other towns they'd passed by or stopped at—where the buildings were crowded together and joined by a wooden boardwalk—Sweetwater Springs was more spread out. Empty lots gapped between several ramshackle structures.

With relief, she saw a brick mercantile on the right and the spire of a white church farther down the street on the left—real signs of civilization.

John turned back to Pamela and held out his free hand. "Ready?"

The crack of gunshots sounded.

Startled by the sound, Pamela let out a shriek, alarm jolting through her. On the far side of the town, a group of mounted riders cantered down the street, guns waving.

Townsfolk raced inside the buildings for cover.

Merciful heavens! She clutched the basket to her chest and whirled to run back to the train.

John cursed and made a grab for Pamela with his free arm, hauling her to his side.

Blood pounding in her ears, she shivered with terror, clutching Smoky's basket to her chest.

"I'll shoot them myself," John muttered in evident fury.

The locomotive blasted the horn, and the wheels began to turn. Panicked that they would miss the train, she struggled to escape. "John, hurry!"

Her husband's arm tightened around her. "It's all right, Pamela. No need to fear."

Gaining momentum, the train pulled away, and she couldn't help a moan escaping.

More gunshots made her flinch.

The sound of hooves thundered. Wheels rattled.

Pamela wanted to bury her face in her husband's shoulder but made herself stand tall and meet danger head on.

A black coach pulled by a team of horses followed the cowboys. The driver snapped a long whip over the heads of the horses. A man driving a wagon brought up the rear.

With no way to escape, Pamela stood stiff within the shelter of her husband's arm, too frozen with fear to even move.

The first of the gunmen pulled his horse to a stop. "Howdy, boss," he called, holstering his gun and dismounting.

The rest of the riders reined in around him.

Boss? John knew these ruffians and ne're-do-wells?

The carriage lumbered to a stop, and the wagon pulled up next to it, followed by clouds of dirt that slowly settled.

"You damn fools!" John thrust the carpetbag at the nearest man.

Bereft of his support, Pamela began to shake, and she thought she might collapse. Horrified visions of beginning her new life by fainting dead away seized her mind.

John rushed to her side and slipped an arm around her back. "Just my men being too stupid to think. They aren't here to hurt us. You're safe."

Slowly the truth seeped in and, not caring they were in public, Pamela lowered her head to John's chest.

She inhaled, grateful her corset strings were loosely tied. Otherwise, her inability to take deep breaths would have made her faint for sure.

John pushed off her hat and deposited a quick kiss on her head, murmuring words, that in her fight to clear her mind, she couldn't quite absorb.

The creak of a floorboard made her startle and look up.

The cowboys ranged in a semi-circle around her, their hats in their hands.

The sight of them so close made her shudder. But Pamela straightened her back and stared at them. These were her husband's men, the fellows who made the ranch run. They might not have the polished manners she was used to, and maybe not a lot of common sense, but they were now her people. *I need to overcome any fear of them.*

One pulled on his forelock. "We sure are sorry, ma'am. We didn't mean to scare you none."

"My men are more brainless than the cattle they herd," John ground out. "I think I'll fire the lot of them and find me some new hands." His eyes glittered with anger.

"Hanging's probably a better punishment," said a gravelly voice from the side of the circle. "Then we won't have to live with the shame of scaring a lady."

Pamela glanced back at the cowboys, this time seeing the true remorse in their eyes. She looked up at John for his reaction.

He glared at the one who'd spoken. "I'll provide the rope and the tree."

She didn't know this hard man who seemed a stranger. *John wouldn't really have them hung, would he?*

Her husband glanced down at her. The stern look in his eyes softened. "Your color is coming back."

"Don't be angry." Pamela's mouth was too dry to make herself heard in more than a whisper.

"I *am* furious, wife, and you can't tell me not to be." John let out a long, slow breath. "But I guess I won't fire them." Shaking his head, he gave a dramatic pause. "Yet."

If Pamela hadn't felt upset, she would have laughed at the hangdog expressions on the men's faces. She managed a weak smile before a shiver coursed through her body.

He pressed a kiss to her forehead. "Chuck, fetch Mrs. Carter some water."

A weathered blue-eyed man slapped his hat against his leg. "Yes, sir. There's a well by the schoolhouse, ma'am. I'll be back as quick as a tail-shake." He took off at a run, the heels of his boots thumping on the wood of the platform.

Tail-shake? She began to sort out the gang of men into individuals, guessing their names based on John's stories.

A man with thick blond hair stared after Chuck.

That one must be Vey.

"Never seen him move so fast," Vey marveled. "Not even when Murphy's dog chased him down the street."

Tears pricked her eyes. She had the oddest need to cry. Pamela sniffed them back. *How ridiculous to well up now! Everything is over, and I'm safe.* But the facts didn't change her response. With all the men watching her, the last thing she wanted was to show weakness. She thought of Elizabeth—her directness, her boldness—and stiffened her spine. With a sense of shame, Pamela realized she had little control over her emotional reaction.

"I'm sorry, my dear." John gentled his voice. "This isn't the homecoming I'd hoped for."

"We was so excited to meet you, ma'am," said an older man with a seamed face and few teeth. "We wanted to give you a real cowboy welcome."

And he must be Frank. Pamela let out a weak laugh. "That you did. You gave me quite a shock."

"You, idiots," John growled, apparently not softened toward them. He squeezed her to him.

"That kind of thing happens, ma'am, when you think you're in *I'm-gunna-die* danger," Vey solemnly assured her. "Afterwards, ya feel as weak as a baby." He shot a sharp look around at the other men, as if daring them to start teasing him.

They all nodded in agreement, and the blond man rocked back on his heels in obvious satisfaction.

Frank gave a sage nod. "'Member that time my horse went down in the river. Snow melt, it was. Swept me away faster than a bullet. Thought I was gunna drown for sure."

Edgar the cook—she could tell by his potbelly—nudged a balding man. "Beans, here saved your sorry a—" he broke off the word, his face and neck reddening. "Ah, bacon, saved your sorry bacon." ·

Frank smirked at the embarrassed man, before turning to

Pamela. "After Beans roped me and dragged me out of the river, thought I was gunna bawl like a baby calf lost from his mama." He nodded. "Yes, siree. I mean. Yes, *ma'am*, I did."

Pamela let out a deep breath. She could see the men's sincere desire to make amends and make her feel better, and she wanted to meet them half way. "This will certainly be a story to write home about."

They all laughed and jostled each other.

Chuck rushed up with a dipper, walking with quick, careful steps, obviously trying to keep from spilling the water.

Pamela schooled herself not to wrinkle her nose at using a communal drinking vessel. With care, she shifted the basket to her left arm and accepted the dipper. "Thank you, Chuck." The water tasted as sweet as John had described, moistening her mouth and quenching her thirst. Just drinking made her feel better. When she finished, Pamela handed the dipper back to Chuck.

Smoky let out a meow, startling the man.

Chuck eyed the basket, his face screwed up in apprehension.

"My cat's in there." Pamela ducked out of John's embrace.

"Meow!"

The men clapped their hats on their heads and parted to form an aisle toward the platform stairs.

As she and John walked through, the scent of horse and unwashed men came her way. Pamela worked hard not to cover her nose.

"Meow, meow."

Beans scooped up her hat and held it out to her.

Pamela smiled a thank you and set it on her head.

"We're almost home, Smoky," she said to the caterwauling kitten. "I'll let you out soon."

John jerked his head at the trunks and crates. "Don't just stand there staring like prairie dogs. Start loading." He leaned over and picked up the carpetbag.

The men jumped to follow his command.

John helped her down the stairs, and they started over to the coach.

With each step, Pamela felt her strength returning until she no longer needed to lean on her husband. She studied the carriage, not remembering any of John's stories featuring one, although he'd spoken often of a wagon. The black body of the vehicle gleamed in the May sunshine. The painted yellow wheels had a light coating of dust. "I didn't know you had a coach."

A smile played around his lips.

Pamela looked at him, her eyes wide. "John Carter, whatever have you done?"

"I bought you a carriage."

She blinked in surprise. "But…"

"But, nothing, wife. I bought the carriage for you to travel in comfort. I didn't want you driving back and forth to town in the wagon. And it's too far for you to ride horseback, tenderfoot that you are," he gently teased. "I ordered it in Boston and had it shipped here as a surprise. I hope you like your wedding gift."

"How did it get here in time?"

"Bought it the day after you said you'd marry me, and the company shipped it out right away."

Touched, she placed her hand on John's arm. Such a practical gift, but romantic as well because the carriage answered her urgent need for safety and provided the comfort she was accustomed to. "Thank you, my dear husband."

Beans stopped short. He carried a long box that she recognized as containing Nick's violin. "Had us widening the road and clearing off any low branches all the way 'tween the ranch and town."

Another man walked by with the trunk containing her hat boxes. The load was light enough to carry by himself. "Filled in the worst of the potholes, too. Although that will probably change with the next big storm."

Beans nodded. "Two whole days it took us. Yes, ma'am, it did. But ain't nothing gunna scratch this pretty carriage of yours."

The man deposited the trunk on the back of the coach.

"Where's Nick?" she asked.

John glanced around as if looking for the boy. Then cocked an eyebrow at Beans. "He stayed back. He's getting Samson all gussied up."

John motioned for her to get inside the coach.

"Let's wait just a few minutes 'til that's loaded." Pamela pointed with her chin to the wagon. "We've been sitting for days."

He nodded his agreement.

When the last box was deposited in the wagon, and everything was lashed tight, John helped her into the coach.

Pamela, basket in hand, slid across the smooth black seats, inhaling the smell of new leather. When John didn't immediately follow her, she leaned forward to peek out the open door.

Her husband stood in quiet-voiced conversation with Digger, the driver. He'd retrieved the carpetbag and held the handle in one hand.

On her side of the coach, she glanced out the window at the men.

"Ain't never seen the boss so angry before," Shoah marveled, checking that a line around the boxes was tight. "Not even when Frank and Beans lost that twenty head of cattle cuz they rode on by the entrance to the ravine where they'd gotten trapped."

John walked over to the coach, thrust the carpet bag on the opposite seat, and climbed inside, shutting the door after him.

Pamela pulled off her hat and tossed it on the other seat. She opened the lid of the basket and took out the kitten, setting him on her lap.

Smoky dug his claws into her dusty gown, then jumped down to the floor and proceeded to explore.

John reached his arm around Pamela's shoulders and pulled her close. "I can't tell you how sorry I am about…"

"It's all right, John."

He shook his head. "I could have strangled each and every one of them."

"I suppose they were excited. But wasn't shooting like that dangerous? If the bullets go up, they must come down."

"I've never heard of anyone being hurt that way. But that doesn't mean it can't happen. Waste of bullets, too, and I supply those to them."

With a tired sigh, she leaned her head against him.

"Just in case they haven't learned their lesson, I'll have a talk with them, lay down the law. No treating guns like fireworks. No shooting one unless there's danger, you're hunting, or you're needing an emergency signal." His body tensed. "And if any man jack of them ever fools around like they did today, he's fired. I don't care how long he's worked for me. I won't tolerate that kind of stupidity." He stopped and took a deep breath, his smile strained. "Guess I'll climb down off my soapbox now."

Smoky stretched and hooked his claws into John's ankle, looked up at him, and mewed..

He reached down and lifted the kitten into his lap.

"Why, John," she teased. "I believe you two are becoming attached."

Giving her a sideways look, he grinned. "I reckon." He ruffled the soft gray fur with his big hand. "If you care for it, I'm bound to."

"*Him*," she corrected with a saucy smile. "Care for him."

"Yep. Guess I'm glad you brought *him* along after all."

Although tempted to make a smug retort, Pamela decided not to rub in her victory. Instead she leaned back, perfectly content to rest in John's arms, watching the scenery—trees mostly, with occasional glimpses of the sky—pass outside the windows.

Sometimes they spoke, but mostly they remained silent.

Pamela wasn't sure how long they'd driven—an hour, maybe two, before the vehicle, which had been steadily climbing, slowed, and then rolled to a stop. She looked a question at him.

"I want to stretch our legs and show you the view of our valley. It's a tradition when we bring someone special to the ranch for the first time." He set the kitten on the seat opposite them and opened the door. He stepped out, then helped her to the ground and started to release her.

Pamela squeezed his hand and didn't let go.

John's quick smile told her he approved. He led her to a lookout and waved an arm in a sweeping motion. "Our valley."

"Really?" Delighted, she leaned forward to take in the view. Grasslands studded with cattle surrounded a big white house, outbuildings, a barn, and two smaller homes. She studied the house. From this distance, it looked large and comfortable, two-story, as John had described, with a porch across the front. She relaxed at the sight.

The distant mountains still held snow on their peaks. Stark blue sky stretched over the land, with several puffy white clouds floating by. *Our valley*, she echoed.

Inhaling a deep breath of crisp air, she leaned against him. "'And I all the while bask in Heaven's blue smile.'"

He cocked an eyebrow. "You have me there."

"Percy Bysshe Shelley. 'The Cloud.' It's in one of the volumes you bought."

Sliding an arm around her waist, he pressed a kiss to her head. "Come, Mrs. Carter. Let's go home."

Nick laid on his bed and stared at the bunkhouse ceiling, one hand petting the dog lying on the floor next to him. He should have gone with the other hands to welcome John home and meet the new Mrs. Carter. But, as much as he looked forward to John's return, he just couldn't bring himself to do so.

After the band of cowboys had set off without him, Nick came to regret his decision. He could almost see his ma—clear as day—standing at the foot of his bed, giving him a tongue-lashing about his manners.

"I cannot believe you're doing a layabout, Nicholas Sanders."

"I didn't want to go," he sullenly answered.

"It's not a matter of what you want. It's a matter of what's right. I didn't raise you to forget your manners the minute I'm gone."

Did he imagine the soft caress across his forehead?

"You'd have grown and gone your own way at some point, my son. But you will always have some part of me and some part of your father inside you. And that includes your manners."

The mental conversation—whether with himself or with a ghost—seemed equally crazy. He sat up, feeling a little foolish, but also having his first sense of comfort since the deaths of his family.

Bandit jumped to her feet and wagged her tail. Earlier, the dog had made it clear by her nudging of his arm and leg that she was puzzled when he came inside and laid down in the middle of the day. She obviously wanted to return to a normal routine.

Normal routine used to mean attending school. Nick shied away from the thought. Now it meant working with the horses. But he'd just finished grooming John's gelding, Samson, until the chestnut coat gleamed in the sunshine. Yesterday, he'd braided the horse's white mane and tail, and today when he'd released the plaits, the long hair waved prettier than a girl's.

Not that the gelding's appearance would deflect John's frustration when he learned the horse had thrush because Shoah was too lazy to clean the hooves properly. And they all were too busy with their own mounts to see that Samson had enough exercise. If Nick hadn't ridden the gelding out last week, he might not have caught the infection in time. But he'd trimmed the frog, scrubbed the entire foot with a stiff brush and warm water, and packed the hoof with iodine-soaked cotton rags. Now, the thrush was clearing up.

Outside the bunkhouse, Nick set his hat on his head and headed for the barn. Over the last few days, a steady stream of crates from Boston had arrived and were piled on the porch. He was pretty sure John's wife would want to get into some of them right away, and for that, they'd need a crowbar. With Bandit at his heels, he fetched one from the workbench in the barn and headed for the ranch house, wondering which of the crates to open first.

But he didn't have a chance to do much thinking on the matter before the sound of wagon wheels and horses' hooves caught his attention.

Bandit raced off, barking.

He set down the crowbar on the porch and hot-footed it after his dog.

The new coach rolled to a stop between the barn and the house. Nick's stomach gave a little dip of excitement. He really had missed John and looked forward to seeing him.

Nick waved to the driver, wondering where the men were. He ran over to the door of the carriage and opened it.

John stepped out. "Nick, my boy." His godfather gave him an unexpected quick hug. "What a sight for sore eyes you are." He turned to reach back inside. "Come, my dear, and meet our Nick." He helped a woman climb out of the carriage.

Howls came from the basket in her arms.

Bandit danced around the woman, anxious to get close to the cat.

John ignored the dog. "This is Pamela," he said to Nick before glancing down at her. "My wife," he said with a proud smile.

Nick didn't know what he expected the new Mrs. Carter to look like. Perhaps something like his own mother with a slender figure and blue-green eyes. John's wife was about Ma's height and definitely female. But there the resemblance ended. For one thing, she wasn't as pretty as his ma. She had a nice face, though. Her cheeks were plump and brown strands of her hair had fallen from a high knot, like she'd just woken up. Not like his mother's smooth wings of dark hair pulled back into a braided bun.

Her clothes were dirty and rumpled, but her tired brown eyes brightened when she saw him. "Goodness, Nick." She shifted the basket and stretched out her hand to him. "John has told me so much about you, I feel as if I know you already." She spoke with a clipped accent, different than the slower Western speech.

He nodded, liking that she was glad to meet him but not at all sure about what to do with her flow of words.

"I understand you're thirteen."

"Fourteen," Nick corrected, knowing he sounded surly. No one on the ranch had remembered his birthday, which took place a few days after the funeral. In fact, he'd done his best to bury any knowledge of the day, for it hurt too much that his family wasn't there to celebrate with him like they always had.

"Damn." John took off his hat and ran a hand through his hair, shorter than before. "I plumb forgot your birthday."

Nick shrugged, but he kept an eye on the new missus to see how she'd react to the curse word. Ma never let Pa, or Nick—or any of the men, for that matter—curse around her, threatening them all with a mouth full of soap.

John shot an apologetic glance at his wife. "Forgive me, Pamela, for my language."

Raising a staying hand, she smiled. "I have three brothers. My ears aren't going to melt if I hear a bad word or two. Though, I'd appreciate if the men of the place—" her gaze touched on Nick "—didn't make a habit of it."

Nick felt a smidge of pride at being counted as one of the men.

John laid a hand on Nick's shoulder and squeezed. "Your ma was the one who always remembered everyone's birthdays. Baked a cake for the special day. Guess none of the rest of us has turned older since she passed. I'm sorry I didn't remember, Nick."

His throat tight, Nick didn't know how to respond.

"I can take on Dora's responsibility," Pamela said in a cheerful tone. "I'll make a list of everyone's birthdays and mark them on the calendar." She touched Nick's arm in sympathy. "I'm not much of a cook, but I do know how to bake a fine cake. What's your favorite flavor?"

John laughed. "Out here, any cake is a treat."

"But everyone has a favorite." Her eyes smiled at Nick. "Well?"

"Chocolate, ma'am." The words surprised him by tumbling out of his mouth.

"Chocolate, it is," she said gaily. "Good thing I brought cocoa powder with me."

John winked at Nick before turning to his wife. "You practically brought all of Boston with you."

"Oh, you." Pamela playfully elbowed his side. "Just you wait. You'll enjoy some of my unexpected treats. Of course, we have a big surprise in store." She gave her husband an imploring look. "Can we please do that today?"

John smiled, his eyes twinkling. "Tonight after supper."

Nick stared in shock. He hadn't seen his godfather look so happy in a long while, not since… He shut away the thought, feeling half resentful, half glad *someone* was feeling better even if he wasn't.

Truth was, John had tried hard all along to be supportive of Nick, even though he could tell the man had his own struggles with grief. If Miz Carter could bring his godfather some ease, who was he to deny the man some comfort?

He tilted his head toward the bunkhouse. "I moved out." Warmth heated the back of his neck. "You all need your privacy."

"Oh, no, Nick. You don't have to do that," Pamela protested with a shake of her head that sent her hair flying. "Please don't leave on my account. I would love the company, being in a new home and all."

"Already done, ma'am." He set his jaw into what Ma had always called his mule look.

She studied him for a moment, compassion in her eyes. "Very well. But if you should change your mind, you are welcome to return and live with us."

Her soft-spoken words thawed his frozen insides just a trickle. "Thank you, ma'am," he said. But Nick knew he wouldn't avail himself of her offer. He was pretty much done with family life.

Chapter Eleven

Pamela told herself not to be hurt by Nick's decision. But she couldn't help feeling rejected by the boy she wanted to mother. *Give him time*, she told herself. *He just met you.*

Nick certainly had beautiful eyes—green with a blue rim around the iris. He had regular features and the kind of fair skin that freckled before tanning, and brown hair that waved to his shoulders.

Pamela made a mental note to offer haircuts to all the men. She wondered if her husband had worn his hair longer before his Boston trip. If he had, Hester would have seen to his grooming upon his arrival.

The black-and-white dog rose on her hind legs to sniff the basket. She had a black band around her eyes, which looked like a mask.

"Down, Bandit." Nick grabbed for her shoulders. "Sorry, ma'am. She's just curious."

"Bandit. An appropriate name." Pamela smiled at Nick. "I have my kitten in the basket. Let's have these two get acquainted, shall we?" She crouched and eased back the lid, although not enough that Smoky would panic and escape.

The kitten blinked in the bright sunlight, then saw the dog. He hissed and arched his back.

Bandit started to thrust her nose inside the basket.

"No, girl." Nick pulled the dog back a few inches. "That critter may be tiny, but he has claws."

Pamela stroked the kitten's head. "Smoky, meet Bandit."

Bandit sniffed and strained to get closer.

Pamela gave the two animals another minute before she stood with Smoky and looked around. She took in the big house with the dormers and broad porch. A stately old oak spread thick limbs and shaded the area. She thought she could see a fenced garden toward the side. "Everything's so peaceful."

John gave a wry twist of his mouth. "That's only because the men aren't here yet. I told them to ride with the wagon. In a few minutes, they'll be here cutting up your peace."

By his gruff tone, she could tell he was still upset with them.

He glanced at Nick. "Darn fools. Rode into town, hoopin', hollarin', and shootin'. Scared Mrs. Carter half to death. Probably the rest of the townsfolk as well. I don't doubt the sheriff will be riding out with a reprimand."

Nick shook his head. "I know they were excited. Didn't have any idea they'd act up though." He glanced at Pamela, his eyes solemn. "I'm sorry that happened to you, ma'am. Not a good welcome to Sweetwater Springs."

A surprised look came over John's face. Wide-eyed, he stared at the boy and shook his head.

With a small smile playing about his mouth, John reached for Pamela's hand. "Why don't you leave Smoky with Nick for now? I'd like to show you around."

Pamela handed over the basket and then took her husband's hand.

John led her away, stopping under the shade of the tree. He glanced behind him, apparently checking to see if the boy was out of earshot, then looked down at her. "Not even here a few minutes, and you've already worked a miracle."

His voice sounded thick with emotion but she wasn't sure why. "Nick?"

"That boy actually had a *conversation*. He spoke a month's

worth of words in five minutes and without first being asked a question." John took her other hand and turned her to face him. "Pamela, words aren't adequate to explain what I feel…" He paused, swallowed, and seemed to consider. "Lighter, somehow?"

"Hopeful?"

"Yes." He gave their joined hands a little shake. "In Boston, I had hopeful *thoughts* of how you being here could make a difference. But now I have hopeful *feelings*."

Her eyes misted, and her heart swelled with love. "I have hopeful feelings, too, John." She faltered. "You don't mind about Nick living in the bunkhouse?"

"I do mind, and I know Dora would have not approved. But I can't have him living alone in their cottage yonder." He gestured to a small house a distance away. "And, as he informed us, he's fourteen. Almost a man. I think I need to respect his choice and hope when he's more comfortable with you that he'll return to us."

After squeezing her hands, he tilted his head toward the house. "Let's go inside."

Up close, Pamela could see the clapboard was in need of whitewashing. In front, weeds sprouted in the flowerbeds bordering the porch. What she could see of the wooden deck not covered from the boxes they'd sent from Boston was scuffed, with only remnants left of the original gray paint. Of the two rockers, one had a frayed cane seat. The windows looked dull and dirty, and the flower boxes in front of them were empty.

So much work to be done. She took a deep breath and mounted the stairs.

The front door had once been painted black and that had faded, too.

John opened the door for her and waited.

She stepped inside, blinking in the dimmer light. The entry looked spacious enough—a hallway with a staircase on the right. A hat rack draped with coats, scarves, and hats stood to her left.

As she walked down the hallway, sand crunched under her feet. She winced, thinking about the additional damage to the already scuffed floors.

John showed her the parlor, with moth-eaten curtains and stiff furniture that looked unused. A layer of dust covered every surface, and a musty odor hung in the air. She hastily backed out.

In the kitchen, an old-fashioned stove was in need of blacking. A rusty splatterware coffeepot perched on one of the burners, a big cast-iron pot on another. Curious, she peered inside and saw beans soaking in water.

"Probably what Edgar's making for supper."

Surely, that's not all he's serving?

She continued her assessment of the kitchen. A brick oven was set into a wall. A filthy scrap of rug lay in front of an outer doorway. The floor was covered with stains, and the big table in the middle of the room had scorch marks and gouges. *This house definitely lacks a woman's touch.*

A long metal sink ran underneath a window that looked on a fenced vegetable garden. *At least, there's a water pump inside.* Pamela hadn't thought to ask John if the house had a bathroom. With a sinking heart, she realized the answer was probably no.

Open shelves held a collection of various-sized bags and tins. Thankfully, they looked well-supplied, if only with staples. "Where's the cellar?"

He pointed to a narrow door she hadn't noticed because it was painted a dingy white like the rest of the woodwork.

Pamela decided she'd brave an inspection of the cellar, which was probably full of spiders and cobwebs, at another time. Striving to keep a smile on her face, she glanced at her husband.

"I'm sorry about the state of the house, Pamela." John shook his head and rubbed a hand over his jaw. "I didn't realize how bad things had grown. I'm afraid, the upstairs isn't much better." He ran his forefinger along a gouge on the table. "After living in beautiful surroundings these past weeks, I see everything with fresh eyes, and I'm downright ashamed."

Pamela took quick steps to his side. "Oh, no, John." She seized his hand with both of hers. "I will admit that the first sight of things daunted me." She let out a shuddering breath and decided to be honest. "On second and third sight, too." She squared her shoulders. "Definitely a lot of work is needed around here to put things to rights."

A relieved expression crossed his face.

Poor man. He must have been dreading my reaction.

"Good thing I brought so much with me. There's plenty of cleaning supplies. But…" She couldn't hold his gaze, almost afraid to make her admission. *What will he think of me?*

"What?" His brow wrinkled into a deep frown. "Tell me, dear."

"In Boston, we had a housekeeper and maids. I've never actually scrubbed anything in my life and wouldn't know where to start."

He chuckled. "I expected that. I saw how you live, servants and all. And Great-Aunt Hester had a frank talk with me. The fact that you can bake a cake is actually an unexpected surprise."

She let out a breath in relief. "Can I count on you and the men to help?"

"Of course. Whatever you need." He chuckled. "Although they might threaten to quit on the spot. And, I have to warn you. I've been away for so long, I don't know what needs doing on the ranch. While you were sitting in the coach in town, Digger told me Samson, you remember that's my gelding, has thrush. I want to go check to see if that hoof was cleaned and properly packed. There's probably a lot more that needs doing with the livestock."

Pamela gave him a reassuring smile. "I'm sure we'll manage," she lied, not sure at all.

Impatient to finish the embarrassing tour of his run-down house and get out to the barn, John showed Pamela the dining and music rooms. Both unused spaces looked as bad as the parlor. His mother had taken such pride in her home, which at one time had been the finest in Sweetwater Springs. If she were still alive, she'd be ashamed of him. Heck, he was ashamed of himself.

With a hand at her elbow, he took Pamela upstairs and decided to first show her the big bedroom—the one they'd be using. He hadn't been inside the room for so long, he couldn't even remember what it looked like, much less what its condition would be. Feeling dread at what he'd find, John opened the door.

Dirty lace curtains framed murky windows. A big four-poster bed was centered in the space. The white featherbed was yellowed and dust covered the furniture—washstand, dressers, wardrobe—as well as dulled the colors of the braided rag rugs on the floor. Even the once copper-colored tile of the fireplace surround looked dull brown.

In silence, Pamela surveyed the room. She walked over and rubbed a circle on the window with the flat of her hand. Then she looked at the palm of her dirty glove with a grimace of disgust and let out a sigh. Leaning close, she glanced outside. "Good thing the days are getting longer. We have a few hours of light left."

He agreed, itching to escape the neglected house, to get out to the barn and check on Samson. Then he wanted to ride out and inspect the cattle.

With a decisive nod, his wife turned back to him. "Here's what we'll do. First, bundle up the bedding and curtains and take them outside. Once you find me a broom and some rags, you can go to see your horse. I'll dust and sweep in here—even *I* can handle those tasks."

"Sounds like a sensible plan," John agreed, glad she was releasing him to go to the barn. He eyed her warily. "You don't plan to tackle the whole house today, do you?"

"Heavens, no. Just the bedroom so we can sleep without breathing dust all night. Please, have one of the men look for a crate labeled *bedding* and open it for me."

"Edgar will handle supper. Don't you worry about that."

She glanced around and brushed her hands together. "After this room is clean and my trunks are brought up, I want to take a bath."

"The tub's in the kitchen. I'll bring it up for you. Might as well start heating the water now so you'll have plenty."

A long sigh escaped, and she gave him a sheepish smile. "A bath will be heavenly."

"Later, I'll go jump in the hot spring."

"Bring all the men and Nick with you," she ordered in a wry tone. "I don't know when they last bathed, but judging from the dirt under their fingernails and their smell..." She wrinkled her nose.

John chuckled. "For some of them, the last washing might have been months ago. We swim in the river on the hot summer days."

Giving a dramatic shudder, she let out a hissing breath of disgust.

"They are grown men, Pamela. I can't order them to bathe."

She fisted her hands on her hips. "But I can!"

A smile tugged at the corner of his mouth. "You surely can, my wife. And that will be a sight to see."

Chapter Twelve

Pamela stepped back and surveyed the bedroom. She'd gotten rid of the worst of the dust on the furniture and floor and had made up the four-poster with the sheets, pillows, and featherbed she'd brought with her. The windows were still dirty, but she'd opened them to let in the fresh air.

Somewhere in the notes that she'd written in a housekeeping journal, now buried in one of her trunks, was the recipe for the concoction she'd need to clean the windows. She'd search for it tomorrow. Now all Pamela wanted was a bath. With longing, she eyed the tin hip tub set in front of the fireplace. John had brought it up earlier and started a fire for her.

The clanging of a bell startled her before she remembered John telling her the sound was the summons to supper. Cleaning the room had taken her longer than she'd expected.

She crossed to the washstand and poured some water from the ewer into the basin. Earlier, Pamela had unpacked the soft towels and French-milled soap she'd brought with her. She picked up the bar and held it to her nose, inhaling the fragrance of orange blossoms. The soap was a wedding gift from her brother Ronald and his wife—enough to last for the next five years.

But even the sweet scent wasn't enough to cover the reek of smoke and dust permeating her hair and clothing. She cast another glance at the washtub, sighed, and left the room.

Pamela followed the sound of male voices to the kitchen and saw the cowboys had gathered around the table. It was set with blue tin splatterware, and there was no cloth protecting the bare wood. She'd brought several heavy linen and lace tablecloths for the dining room, but this room needed something simple. She mentally started a list of things she'd need Elizabeth to send her.

Edgar stood at the stove, stirring a pot. He gave her an embarrassed look. "Ah, since I was gone to town for so long I didn't have a chance to cook. We're just having a plain supper. Eggs and beans. There's bread I made yesterday and store bought butter and jam."

Didn't all butter and jam come from a store? Even as she thought the question, Pamela realized how ridiculous it was.

Edgar smiled, showing yellowing horse teeth. "But now that you're here, we can have fresh butter. The berries will be ripe soon, and you can start canning."

Pamela shot John a panicked glance. She didn't know how to make butter or can berries. And she knew for a fact that the instructions weren't written down in her notebook. It obviously hadn't occurred to her cook and housekeeper that she wouldn't be buying butter and jam.

"No need to get ahead of yourself, my dear." John's smile reassured her. "We can keep the Cobbs in business for a while longer."

She wrinkled her brow. "The Cobbs?"

"Shopkeepers," Frank said, with a gap-tooth grin. "Mr. Carter, here, keeps on their good side by spending money in their place."

"Not the most hospitable people, but they keep the mercantile well-stocked." John walked over to the foot of the table. "You'll have your hands full enough with setting this house to rights. The rest will come in time." He pulled out a chair for her.

Although she was relieved by the reprieve, Pamela couldn't shake the overwhelmed feeling weighing her down. *So much work! So much to learn!*

Pamela allowed John to seat her.

With a shy smile for her, Nick took a seat at John's right.

She bowed her head while her husband said grace and helped pass around the bowls of food so everyone could help themselves—another custom she wasn't used to.

The cowboys dug in with an appetite, eating as if they hadn't seen food for years.

She turned her eyes away from the men with the worst manners and wondered if there was a way to politely teach them better ones. Hunger prompted her to eat, even though she found the plain fare rather bland. The dark bread was heavy, but probably more substantial for hard working men than the lighter white bread she was accustomed to.

When the cowboys had polished off every bit of food, Pamela cleared her throat. "Gentlemen…I'm sure you know my presence here will bring about some changes." She glanced around the table with a warm smile. "Hopefully, you'll find many of them for the better."

They gave her smiles and nods in return. "I'm new to the West, new to housekeeping, and I'll have to ask you all to bear with me until I get my feet under me. I'm a…" She thought of the word she'd heard John use several times. "Greenhorn."

Her husband smiled and raised his coffee cup to her.

"Now one of the changes I'd like to implement is cleanliness. I'm told there's a hot spring here that's perfect for soaking. I'd like you all to bathe tonight, including washing your hair. I've brought along soap that I think you will like—smells like bay leaves. It's what my father and brothers use."

The men stared at her.

Nick wouldn't meet her eyes.

Beans grinned and nodded, but the rest didn't look at all convinced. A few glanced at their boss for his reaction.

John held up his hands in a gesture of surrender. "I've used that bay soap while I was in Boston, too. After the long journey, I intend to avail myself with a bath. I'd like you all to make my wife happy by joining me."

Old Frank shook his head. "No disrespect, Miz Carter, but my ma always said bathing lets the ill-humors in. I've lived me a long life by listening to her advice."

Pamela had never heard of such a thing and had no idea what to say. She glanced at John for inspiration.

Her husband just shrugged, a small turn of his mouth indicating he was enjoying this discussion.

But Pamela knew she had his support, and his belief in her strengthened her resolve.

A few of the men gave Frank uneasy looks, then slid their gazes to her and back again.

Nick pushed his plate away. "I'll take a bath with you, John." He shot a sharp glance at Frank. "*My* ma took great store in us being clean. I've let her down, I'm ashamed to say."

An uneasy silence followed his words. By evoking his deceased mother, Nick had just backed everyone of them into a corner.

Frank scowled.

Before the older man could say anything that would cement his opposing position, Pamela jumped into the conversation, sweetening the deal so to speak. "I've brought chocolate from Boston as a special treat—European chocolate, the best!" She waited for that to sink in before continuing. "After everyone's bathed, we're going to have a little dessert party to celebrate our homecoming. And, John and I have brought presents for all of you."

Her husband winked at her. "Guess we're celebrating Christmas in May."

His remark made everyone sit up, eager expressions on their faces.

Pamela put a hint of steel into her tone. "I will see everyone back here in about two hours for chocolate and presents...*bathed* and wearing their best clothes."

Hatless and with their hair still damp, the men converged on the kitchen, smelling like bay leaves and the cedar from the wooden chest in the bunkhouse where their best clothes were stored.

Nick's good shirt was too tight in the shoulders, and his wrists hung out. The pant hems hitched up a couple of inches, too, making some of the hands joke about needing to put rocks on his head to stop him from growing. He didn't mind the teasing, though. Felt like old times. Good times, making him hopeful that better times might come again, hard as that was to believe.

The men had whiled away their bath by joking about their presents, making outlandish bets on what they each might receive. All the while, John had remained silent, listening but with a light in his eyes—the same contented gleam his godfather had displayed since arriving home with his new wife.

Despite Frank's objection, all the men found themselves in the pool where the hot spring flowed out and cooled enough to bathe. The old man was the single holdout, sitting fully-clothed on a nearby rock.

But Frank only lasted until John broke his silence. He began to describe the European chocolate—the food of angels, he called it—waiting for them upon their return to the house. The heavenly beings must have trumped Frank's ma, for lickety-split the man shucked off his clothes and gingerly slid into the steaming pool.

They'd all took turns washing their bodies and hair with the soap, and sat and soaked. The water felt so good on tired muscles, more than one of the men asked why they didn't do this more often.

With the new missus around, Nick had no doubt they'd frequently find themselves in this hot spring. Mrs. Carter would probably be like his ma, insisting on baths every Saturday night, but also after having completed a smelly chore like delivering a foal. Swishing his hands through the water, Nick decided he wouldn't mind too much.

Anxious to have chocolate—a rare treat—and see what presents the Carters had brought from Boston, Nick pulled ahead of the pack coming from the bunkhouse and trotted up the back steps to the kitchen, anticipation lending a spring to his steps.

He burst through the door and stopped short at the sight of Miz Carter clad in a shiny reddish gown, with the same color jewelry glinting at her neck and ears. John, wearing a new suit, stood next to her. The couple appeared so elegant that Nick had to blink a few times to be sure who they were.

He let out a slow breath and tried to pull down his sleeves, to no avail.

"Come in, Nick." Her smile was warm, and her eyes sparkled like her jewels.

The other men clattered into the kitchen and had a similar brought-up-short reaction to the sight of the Carters' finery.

Mrs. Carter beamed at the group. "Gentlemen, how handsome you all look."

Nick had once heard his ma say that John's cowboys were a homely lot, and he didn't think some soap and water would make much of a change to that fact.

But the men puffed out their chests as if they believed her and ducked their heads in acknowledgment.

Biting back a smile, Nick stored away their peacocking reactions, certain he could find a chance in the future to tease them.

She waved toward the table. "Sit, gentlemen."

Two oil lamps burned on both sides of a platter of gold and silver foil-covered circles. Packages wrapped in tissue paper lay on each plate. Nick glanced from the table to John and cocked an eyebrow.

John grinned, holding his hands palms up. "I know what's in

the packages because I bought them, but I don't know anything else about this party. Mrs. Carter was a busy bee before she left Boston."

Eyes wide and expressions curious, the ranch hands all took their accustomed seats, giving Miz Carter expectant looks.

Across the table, husband and wife shared a long glance before she looked at the men. "Go ahead." She waved her hand. "Open them."

Nick ripped apart his parcel to find a new blue shirt and smiled. *No more bare wrists for me!*

The rest of the men tore into their packages, then apparently stricken speechless at their new shirts, stared at the garments in awe.

Frank ran a tentative hand over his red flannel shirt. "I'm sure glad I washed up for this."

Everyone burst into laughter.

Nick held his blue shirt up to himself, stretching out his arm. The sleeve length more than covered his wrists and the beginning of his hand.

"Think I couldn't pick the right size?" John teased.

"Don't need any more small shirts," Nick retorted.

John's smile widened, the corners of his eyes crinkling. "We have more clothes for you, to replace what you've grown out of."

Overwhelmed by their kindness, Nick looked down, struggling to retain some of the protective aloofness he'd felt before Miz Carter's arrival. "Thank you."

The men also murmured quiet thanks, their voices full of gratitude.

Mrs. Carter lifted the platter in front of her and, with her thumb and forefinger, picked up a gold chocolate and set it on her plate. "The gold ones are plain chocolate, and the silver ones have cherry flavor inside. Every man gets one of each." She passed around the platter. When everyone had taken their pieces, she unwrapped the first candy

Given tacit permission, the men followed her lead.

Nick took small bites, savoring each melting morsel. He'd never tasted anything so wonderful.

John pushed back from the table, rose, and walked out of the kitchen. He returned in a minute, carrying a cloth-wrapped bundle that he placed in Nick's arms.

"Your parents had plans to get you this for Christmas. To my sorrow, I didn't think to follow through on their intention sooner. However, when I first told Mrs. Carter about you, she suggested this gift." He motioned to the bundle. "Go ahead."

The thought of his parents sent a jolt through Nick. With shaking hands, he unwrapped the cloth to uncover a shiny new violin. Struck silent with awe, he ran his fingertips over the smooth surface of the reddish wood and plucked one of the strings.

John handed him the bow, which he'd been hiding.

Stunned, Nick stared down at the beautiful violin his parents had wanted for him.

"Do you like it?" John asked.

Nick nodded. He could feel the weight of everyone's expectations pressing on him. He knew they wanted him to pick up the instrument and play some music. And, indeed, he wanted to, as well. But he couldn't, for a fresh wave of grief seized him, and his arms felt as leaden as his heart. He swallowed a couple of times but couldn't even push words of gratitude from his tight throat.

In the silence, he heard the scrape of a chair press back and light footsteps coming his direction. But he didn't look up, not even when he smelled Miz Carter's perfume and felt her hand on his shoulder.

"It's all right, Nick. We understand. You don't have to play that violin until you're ready."

Although her words were meant to comfort, all they did was send him deeper into despair, for Nick wasn't sure he'd ever be ready to make music without his family to hear him play.

Chapter Thirteen

The next morning, Pamela stood at the bedroom window, feeling refreshed after a long night's rest, and watched a drizzle mist the dirty panes of glass. Last night, she'd gone to bed while John walked to the bunkhouse with Nick, and she'd fallen asleep before his return. She'd also slept through his rising and was anxious to see him.

Out of habit, she dabbed perfume on her neck and wrists. Silly, perhaps, to wear scent when she'd be working like a laborer. *But I'm still a new bride…*

She donned a brown work dress and ruefully surveyed herself in the mirror over the washstand. The garment that had seemed so plain and simple in Boston, here in Montana was too fine to subject to the damages of her work day. Now she regretted leaving her old gardening clothes behind. *But at least I've brought an apron,* she consoled herself. *I just need to find where Jean packed it.*

Pamela thought of her traveling clothes, bundled up and thrust out onto the porch, and wondered if somehow she could salvage them. Then she realized she didn't have notes in her journal on how to do laundry. She wracked her mind, trying to recall the times when she'd watched the maids.

Shaking her head at her own ignorance, she made the bed, another chore she hadn't done before the previous night. At least this was a task she could easily figure out. As she pulled the sheets straight and fluffed up the pillows, she found a piece of paper crammed between them.

John must have left her a note and it had fallen off. Eagerly, she began to read.

Pamela,

This morning, I wanted to stay in our warm bed, feel you in my arms, and smell the scent of orange blossoms in your hair. But I forced myself to leave without waking you.

The life of a rancher means early mornings. I know you've had an exhausting week and there's more to come, so your rest is important.

I'll see your sweet face later.

Your loving husband,

John

With a thrill, she lingered on the words *sweet face* and *your loving husband*, then reread the message. When she finished, Pamela pressed the note to her chest and said a quick prayer of thanksgiving. In spite of a run-down, dirty house and a bunch of rough cowboys to whip into order, she was so happy she'd married John Carter. *He sounded as if he was glad he married me, too.* While he seemed to be content with his marriage, sometimes doubts still niggled.

A knock sounded at the door.

She crossed the room to open it and found her husband smiling at her, a tray of breakfast food in his hands.

"Good morning, Pamela. The men have eaten and gone. I've brought you some tea and toast. I hope Edgar made the poached egg the way you like it."

"I just found this." She waved the letter at him. "Such a lovely message. Thank you."

"I just wish I could have told you in person."

"I'm sure I'll adapt to getting up early."

"In time, my dear. In time."

Pamela took the tray from him and set it on the dresser. The fragrance of her favorite beverage wafted her way. She looked at him in inquiry. "I didn't unpack the tins of tea."

John laughed and pulled her to sit on the bed next to him, giving her a kiss. "You're not the only one who can plan ahead, my dear," he teased.

She melted against him. "Oh, John."

"You smell good."

Inside she thrilled at his compliment. "How's Samson?"

"Nick's done a good job. I think the thrush should be cleared by next week."

"And the rest of the livestock?" She tried to sound like the knowledgeable wife of a rancher.

"I'm torn between riding out to check on the herd and staying to ease my bride into her new life. Then there's my godson...."

Sadness entered his eyes, and the corners of his mouth turned down.

"What is it?"

"There's something else I planned for…that I think is a good idea, but I'm not sure."

Concerned, she placed her hand over his. "Tell me."

"The Sanders family is buried in the cemetery by the church in town. But that's a far piece for a boy to go if he has a hankering to pay his respects."

She waited for him to continue.

"We have a graveyard here. My parents and grandparents lie there. My…" he shook his head. "Some of my ranch hands, too. I wanted a memorial for Nick that would be close by—one he could walk to when he feels the urge. I know that sometimes I just need to go and visit with my loved ones."

Remembering her visits to her mother's grave, Pamela nodded.

"While in Boston, I had a memorial plaque made for the Sanders family. I thought I'd fasten it to one of the trees."

"You are the *most* thoughtful man," Pamela said, a catch in her throat. "Would you like me to come with you, or would the two of you prefer to be alone?"

"Given how Nick has warmed up to you, I'd like you to be there. I thought we could go after you eat and before you get deep into cleaning and whatnot. Then I need to get back to work."

"He's struggling so, poor boy. It just wrings my heart. Why, I thought I was going to burst into tears last night."

"Not the way I expected him to receive the violin." John gave his head a slow shake. "Guess I shouldn't have mentioned that part about his parents."

She squeezed his hand. "You did the right thing. Nick might have a hard time accepting the instrument, but in time, that violin will have even more meaning for him."

John let out a sigh. "I hope so."

Pamela leaned forward to kiss his cheek. "Mark my words, John Carter." She waved him toward the door. "Go get Nick. I'll be down in a few minutes."

John strolled with Pamela and Nick to the graveyard, situated far enough from the house for privacy, but close enough for a body to go and sit a spell. The rain had stopped, and the overhead clouds had lightened. He carried a bag containing the metal plaque wrapped in a pillowcase, a hammer, and four nails. The three of them were quiet as they walked, although Pamela glanced around with bright-eyed curiosity. John just couldn't shake his concern about Nick's reaction to the plaque enough for conversation.

Nick's face looked drawn, and he moved stiffly as if his body ached.

John couldn't help remembering the carefree boy of six

months ago—the one he'd glimpsed yesterday upon their arrival—and hoped Nick's back-and-forth grieving would have more forward momentum in the future.

He checked on Pamela, who held her skirt a few inches above the damp grass. Even with his worry about his godson, John savored the simple act of walking over his land with a *wife*. And not just any wife—his beloved Boston bride.

Pamela wore a brown straw hat adorned with a tan ribbon. Her simple although stylish dress made her appear like an Eastern version of a Western housewife.

They passed the Sanders' small vacant house. Dried leaves had gathered on the porch, and dust obscured the windows. Undaunted by the surrounding weeds, a rose bush climbed over the porch rail, the red blooms bright against the gray paint. By habit, both Nick and John looked away.

"What beautiful roses." Pamela slowed her steps. "Does anyone live there?" She glanced from John to Nick, and comprehension dawned on her face. "This was your family's house, wasn't it?"

Nick nodded, not meeting her eyes.

"It's a lovely place," she said, understanding warmth in her voice. "Your mother must have loved her home." She paused as if waiting for his response. "Perhaps, when we have some time, we can wash the windows and weed the garden. Would you like that? Probably the inside needs dusting, too." Pamela tried to banter with the boy. "I speak from recent, intimate experience with dust."

Nick obliged with a dutiful smile, but even that was more of a response than John had gotten out of the boy in the last months—barring yesterday, of course.

"Do you attend school, Nick?" Pamela asked, seemingly undaunted by his lack of response.

School! His wife's innocent question hit him in the gut. Between grieving and the press of ranch work, made even more difficult without his foreman, John had completely forgotten about school. He wanted to groan and bury his head in shame. Up in heaven, Dora must be having a conniption fit. She'd always pushed Nick to succeed. *I'm falling down on the job of being a parent.*

"No, ma'am," Nick said in a low voice.

Pamela's brow furrowed. "Why is that? I'm sure I saw a schoolhouse in town."

"You did," John answered, his voice grim. "In winter, the children around here study at home. Then we had the branding, but after that...? Nick, why didn't you say something?"

The boy shrugged, sullenness radiating from his stooped posture.

"Well, I'm to blame." John shot Nick a stern glance. "Starting Monday, no more shirking your schooling."

Nick nodded, his closed expression giving no hint of his feelings.

"I imagine the bunkhouse can be a noisy place," Pamela commented, with a reproving glare at John that belied her tactful tone. "After supper each night—" she said to Nick "—I'd like you to stay at the big house so you can study for a few hours in peace. John and I brought many books from Boston, so that can be our quiet reading time, too."

Nick didn't say anything, he simply gave her a polite smile.

John wanted to smack his forehead. *Of course, Nick was avoiding school!* The whole idea must have been too painful, reminding him of his mother. Then, too, for the last year, the boy had been solely responsible for his sister traveling to and fro with him. "You're a mighty smart young man." He softened his voice. "I know you'll catch up on what you've missed in no time. We'll see that you do, Mrs. Carter and I. We'll help you."

They reached the circle of trees that surrounded the graveyard. Grass dotted with wildflowers grew in the clearing. Engraved headstones designated the family graves on the left. The ranch hands were on the right, their graves marked by simple wooden crosses carved with their names. An apple tree, planted by John's grandfather after his wife's death, grew next to their double headstone. The branches, covered with white flowers that shivered in the breeze, sheltered his grandparents' graves.

As always, John avoided the space between his parents' resting site where his sister lay.

Nick looked around the area, then glanced at John in inquiry.

He hadn't told the boy why he wanted him to come with them. Still questioning if this was a good idea, John held out the bundle. "This is for you. Well, not the hammer and nails. But another gift, perhaps even more painful than the violin," he warned. "Like the instrument, I hope at some point it will also bring you comfort."

The breeze kicked up, rustling the leaves of the trees and wafting the scent of grass their way. The brim of Pamela's hat fluttered, and she reached up to adjust the ribbon, pulling down the ends to tie them under her chin.

Nick opened the bag, pulled out the bundle, and unwrapped the plaque. Silently, his shoulders hunching, he read the engraving:

IN LOVING MEMORY OF
Andrew Sanders
Dora Sanders
Marcy Sanders

"He spake well who said that
graves are the footprints of angels."

Henry Wadsworth Longfellow

Pamela tensed beside him.

John sensed she was ready to intercede if needed, although he didn't know what she could do.

Head bowed and eyes closed, Nick clutched the plaque to his chest, letting the bag swing from his other hand.

John braced himself for some emotion, tears perhaps, but the boy's calmness surprised him.

Nick let out a long, slow breath and straightened. With a slight smile, he nodded. "This is good." He paused for a long moment, as if considering whether to speak more. "It's weighed on me, them not being close."

Guilt stabbed him. "I'm sorry, son. The accident took place so near to town. Their bodies were taken there… They're buried next to your grandparents and your uncle." John placed a hand on Nick's shoulder. "Many good reasons for the decision, but I should have thought—"

"No. I like that they're in Sweetwater Springs with family and by the church. Ma sure did like going to town. Marcy loved school."

John let out a breath of relief. "Well then. How 'bout you pick a tree to hang this on?"

Nick took his time circling the edge of the graveyard and studying each tree.

Pamela touched John's arm. "That went well."

"I'm surprised. Pleased and surprised. Gives me hope."

Nick gestured, and they followed him over to a pine. "There's space between those two branches. I could cut away the dead ones later to show it more." He pointed toward the lower limbs.

"Looks like a good choice."

While they figured out which branches needed to be lopped off, Pamela wandered over to read the headstones.

With them working together, only a few minutes were needed to finish nailing the plaque to the tree. They stepped back to admire their handiwork.

Nick worked his jaw as if he was holding back tears.

He hesitated. The boy was so *distant*, and John didn't want to do the wrong thing—make matters worse. But an inner prompt made him drop the hammer, throw an arm around Nick's shoulders, and pull him against his side.

For a moment, the boy resisted, his body stiff. Suddenly, he melted, flinging his arms around John's waist and holding on hard.

A lump rose in John's throat. "I miss them too, Nick…think of them every day. And, I've hurt for you, boy. I feel like you're my own son, and I haven't…haven't been able to let you know how much you mean to me. How I hurt to see you suffer alone."

Nick stepped back, mopped his eyes with his sleeve. "I don't know what I'd do without you, John."

Had the boy feared I would abandon him? Surely not. But just in case, the words need saying. "You won't have to. I'll always be there. And now Mrs. Carter will, too."

John gazed over at Pamela who watched them with tear-filled eyes. His wife radiated love and compassion, and she'd never been so beautiful to him.

Nick released a long sigh. He glanced at the plaque and gave a little nod. Then he stooped and picked up the hammer. "I'll take this back to the barn."

Out of the corner of his eye, John saw his wife's proud smile.

Pamela turned away to move along the graves. She stopped at Sarah's headstone and read the inscription.

John tensed, bracing himself for the questions to come.

His wife glanced over, a troubled expression on her face.

Nick followed John's gaze and saw where Pamela was standing. He glanced up at John. "Tell her."

John looked into his godson's green eyes and saw wisdom beyond the boy's years reflected back. Andrew and Dora surely had told him about Sarah because Nick had never heard the story from John. *No one has.*

"I'll be going." Nick raised the hammer.

Now it was John's turn to thank his godson, an odd dance of grief and appreciation.

Nick nodded and left.

Slowly, John joined his wife.

She took his hand and squeezed. "I think maybe Nick has turned a corner today. Both of you have."

John stood next to her and looked down at the headstone. He couldn't bear to read his sister's name, but he forced himself to look anyway.

Sarah Katherine Carter
Beloved daughter of Katherine and Daniel Carter,
and sister of John
1857-1863

He'd never read the inscription before. Didn't know his parents had added the part about him.

"You've told me plenty of stories," Pamela said softly. "But nothing about your sister."

He didn't meet her gaze, his chest tight. "I couldn't."

"Why?"

Such a simple question. "I'd taken Sarah fishing. She'd been begging me for days, little pest that she was."

"I know about pesky little sisters."

He crouched and traced the word *beloved* with one finger. "I didn't realize how much she meant to me until she was gone."

"I remember that kind of remorse, as well."

"Finally, I gave in to her pleading." For so long, John had held the memory distant, and he told the story in a monotone. "My mother was pleased that I'd agreed to spend time with her. But since she'd recovered from being ill a few weeks earlier, Ma sternly warned us that Sarah was *not* to go into the water. She made me promise to keep a close watch on her."

"Let me guess. Sarah got wet." Pamela patted his arm.

"Yep. Became too excited when she caught a trout, reeled it in, leaned over to pick up the fish, a big one, and it slipped out of her hands. She grabbed for it and over balanced. I pulled both her and the fish out of the water. That fish flapped all over her," he said with a hint of a smile.

"You two must have been drenched."

"We were scared we'd get in trouble. It was a hot day, anyway, but I figured a fire would hurry things along. If Sarah was dry by the time we returned home, our mother would never know."

"Did you keep fishing?"

"Of course. I hadn't been prohibited from getting wet, so I didn't need to dry out. And, I was miffed that my little sister had caught one before me. I wandered downstream and out of eyeshot, although I heard her singing and playing. I don't know what happened. I just heard her scream…and scream." He passed a shaky hand over his face. "The sound haunts me still."

"I can only imagine," Pamela murmured in sympathy.

"I raced to her. Her dress was on fire and instead of heading toward the water, Sarah instinctively ran toward home. Yelling for her to stop, I chased her, but by the time I tackled her and beat out the flames, she was badly burned."

As Pamela listened, her hand crept to her mouth. Tears welled up and began to fall as she grieved for the death of the little girl and the brother who lost her and obviously blamed himself.

"I tried to pick her up and carry her home, but Sarah was too heavy. Though I hated to, I had to leave her and run for help." He shook his head. "She died three days later."

Pamela couldn't speak.

Something broke inside John, and the old feelings of terror and guilt swamped him. He gasped with pain.

Needing to offer what comfort she could, Pamela wrapped her arms around him and held him while the feelings raged and only slowly ebbed.

Shaken, John turned and saw her wet cheeks. "Pamela." He cupped her face with his hands and brushed away her tears with his thumbs. "Sarah died a long time ago."

"Sometimes, an old loss hurts as much as if it happened yesterday." She reached up and placed her hands over his. As her fingers touched his palms, she felt the ridges of his scars. She pulled down his arms and turned his hands over, studying his palms. "I didn't realize you'd been burned, too. I thought this was just from ranch work."

"Would that it were," he said bitterly.

"Oh, John." Her voice was soft with understanding. She brought first one hand, then the other to her lips, kissing the scars and wishing she could make his pain go away.

She glanced toward the graves. "Did your parents blame you?"

"They never said so. But how could they not?"

"You were what? Nick's age?"

"About that. Maybe a little younger."

"Would you have blamed Nick if Marcy had died under his care?"

He closed his eyes, and with a sharp inhale, tilted back his head.

She waited.

Exhaling, John opened his eyes and looked at her. "No. No, I wouldn't."

"Then think of that boy you were, and don't blame yourself."

He brought her to him for a heartfelt hug and buried his face in her hair. "Such a wise woman."

They remained in the embrace until John pushed back so he could see her expression.

"Guess that's why I never married before Nick's situation forced me."

"What do you mean?"

"I've always been afraid a tragedy would happen again. That I couldn't protect a wife, a daughter." He confessed his deepest fear, then grabbed a fold of her skirt and shook it. "All this loose material can be dangerous."

She raised her eyebrows.

"If I had a daughter…a wife…and I couldn't save her." John's voice dropped as he shared his secret. "It's my greatest nightmare." His gut heated, and his breathing rasped just imagining the horror of such an occurrence.

With a quick nod, Pamela placed a hand on his arm. "Well then, we'll just have our daughter wear trousers."

Her unexpected answer uttered in a practical tone was like a dash of cold water. He'd never thought of such a simple solution. "You'd do that?"

"Well, not to church. But certainly when she's on the ranch."

A trickle of humor penetrated the pain. "What about you…?"

She raised her chin. "If I'm to be around an open campfire, then yes, I shall wear trousers, too." She sent him a narrow-eyed look as if daring him to laugh.

"I've never told anyone the story. Never talked about Sarah. Kept the memory locked tight away." He clenched his jaw.

Pamela placed her hands on each side of his face. "In the days to come, I want to hear more about Sarah. I'm sure you have plenty of stories." And she drew him down for a kiss.

Chapter Fourteen

John and Pamela strolled back to the house in companionable silence. Pamela lifted her face to the sky, enjoying the feel of the sun that had broken through the clouds, the fresh air, her bucolic surroundings. She couldn't fathom that all this land belonged to her husband, and that someday future generations of her bloodline would walk these same acres—feeling, she supposed, a similar sense of pride and awe.

As they'd stood before his sister's grave and talked, something had shifted between them. Or perhaps, it would be more accurate to say something had shifted within John—old pain and guilt and fear. She wasn't naive enough to think that his troubles from Sarah's death had vanished. Or that the specter of John's fear wouldn't again rear its monstrous head. But Pamela had a feeling her husband would now be able to face his demons and slay them.

What about mine? She thought of her beloved little sister and realized that she might have envied the attention Mary received for being pretty and talkative. Perhaps she, too, harbored guilt from the past.

Pamela heard the sound of hoofbeats and wagon wheels. She glanced up to see a buggy, followed by several riders, and then some wagons, descending the road from the mountain pass. "What is going on?" She glanced over at her husband.

As he squinted toward the riders, John wore a puzzled expression. "I don't know."

"They must be coming to pay us wedding visits. It hadn't occurred to me that this far away from town, we'd have callers."

He frowned.

A wave of shyness overcame her. Of all things she disliked— being among a group of people she didn't know. *Everyone will be watching me, judging me.* The thought made her uncomfortable, but… Pamela straightened her shoulders. She was well-trained in being a gracious hostess, no matter how she felt.

She brought herself up short. "Oh, dear Lord. The house isn't in any state to be seen. And what will we feed them?"

John shook his head. "We'll figure it out." He placed his hand in the small of her back and guided her toward the barn. "Guess you'll have that opportunity to dazzle the neighbors sooner than we thought."

"How, pray tell?" she said tartly, waving a hand down her body. "I'm hardly dressed for company."

In spite of the frantic thoughts of dealing with so many visitors that skittered through her brain, she enjoyed the way his slow grin and up and down appraisal sent heat rushing into her cheeks.

"Ya look mighty purty to me, wife," he drawled.

At the sound of the broadest Western twang she'd ever heard him use, Pamela rolled her eyes and laughed.

By the time they'd reached the area in front of the barn, the first buggy had come to a stop.

"The Nortons," John said in a low voice.

"Ah, the minister and his wife."

He smiled. "Yep. Good memory. And their son?"

"Joshua." Pamela tilted up her chin in triumph. "He's to attend the seminary in the fall."

"Excellent, Mrs. Carter."

By the time they'd reached the Norton family, Pamela realized their bantering had helped settle her nerves. *Probably as John intended.*

Reverend Norton set the brake on the buggy and waved hello.

Joshua jumped down and reached up to help his mother climb out. Then he lifted a basket from the floor.

"Welcome." John greeted them.

Mrs. Norton smiled and glanced between the couple.

She was a small woman who wore her brown hair in a plain, tight bun, and her dress was far shabbier than the ones Pamela had left behind in Boston. Suddenly, she didn't feel as insecure about her own appearance.

"You're probably wondering what we're doing here," Mrs. Norton said in a gentle voice.

"Always glad to see you," John said in a friendly tone.

"We've come to help."

"Help?" John's eyebrows shot up in surprise.

Mrs. Norton smiled at Pamela and stepped forward to pat John's arm. "Because that is what we do in Sweetwater Springs—we help each other out."

Nick, who'd been scrubbing out the horse trough, rushed forward to unharness the Norton's horse.

"But I don't need help," John said, still sounding bewildered. He drew Pamela forward. "May I present my wife, Pamela."

"Nonsense," Reverend Norton said in a booming voice, striding to them. He nodded to Pamela. "We are blessed to have you join our community, Mrs. Carter." He gave John a disapproving frown. "This place is falling to rack and ruin."

"Yes, but—"

"You've just brought home a bride," the minister interrupted with a stern tone and a sideways glance at Pamela.

The man had intense blue eyes in an austere bearded face. He looked like a Biblical prophet in modern—albeit, shabby—clothing. "A ranching life will be enough of an adjustment for a fine lady without her having to wear herself out fixing up the place when she first sets foot onto it." The man swept his arm in an encompassing gesture.

In spite of her panic at the thought of a horde of people descending on her, Pamela couldn't help a bubble of amusement as her normally unflappable husband looked like a fish just netted and tossed upon the land.

The minister turned and pointed to indicate the trail of people on the road. Like ants boiling out of an anthill, more vehicles crested the hill and spilled down the slope. "You can't deny, John Carter, that you've aided many people, many times. And your parents and grandparents before you."

Mrs. Norton reached for a basket held by her son, Joshua.

At about age sixteen or so, the boy looked like a weedy replica of his father, including the vividness of his eyes. But Pamela judged he'd soon fill out and grow into an attractive man.

"Now don't you worry, Mrs. Carter, about hospitality and food," Mrs. Norton said in a soothing voice. "We're well used to pot luck, and every family will bring something." With a smile, she lifted up the basket. "I've two loaves of fresh baked bread."

"Why, thank you, Mrs. Norton." With a feeling of relief, Pamela held out her hands for the basket.

The woman evaded her reach. "No, no, dear. I know where the kitchen is. You go greet the rest of your guests."

"Yes, John," Reverend Norton agreed. "Introduce your bride to everyone."

He squinted at the family in a wagon pulling up next to the Nortons' buggy. Riders surrounded them.

"The Addisons with their son, Donny. Can't remember their girls. Their cowboys are riding along with them." He pulled his brows together. "Looks to me like they brought all their hands."

The Addisons were spare and brown—hair, eyes, tanned skin. They quietly greeted Pamela, mentioning they were the Carters' nearest neighbors.

The next family was memorable for the gang of boys riding in the wagon bed. Beside the parents, their pretty blond daughter sat in the midst of the bunch like their crown jewel. The boys jumped out almost before the vehicle came to a stop and scattered in several directions.

A tall, roman-nosed young man tenderly helped the young lady out of the wagon.

"Wyatt Thompson," John said in a low undertone. "Engaged to Alicia. He's new around here. Bought the ranch next biggest to mine in size. Run-down place."

She raised her eyes at the irony of that statement.

"Not like here," John said with a touch of exasperation. "I run a good spread, Pamela, even if I neglected my house."

"Of course, John," Pamela teased, then turned her attention back to her guests. She didn't think handsome Mr. Thompson looked old enough to be the owner of a large ranch until she was introduced to him and saw the world-weary wariness in his gray eyes.

"Here come the Cobbs." John's tone held a warning. A well-dressed couple in their thirties sauntered over, their attitude proclaiming they expected to be accorded respect. They looked to be an odd match—he tall and balding with a bulbous nose, she short and plump with close-set eyes. But both gazed at her with the same calculating gleam.

"We're the Cobbs," the woman announced in a self-important tone.

Mr. Cobb waved toward the house. "We've brought cans of paint and brushes."

"That's mighty kind of you," John said with a nod of acknowledgment.

"We've put the sum on your account."

Pamela suppressed a smile and echoed her husband's thanks.

By this time, so many riders and wagons had arrived that Pamela was overwhelmed by introductions. Each family, along with their cowboys or other workers, moved forward to greet the newlyweds, bringing tools, food, cleaning supplies, and small gifts.

Something about the way the people presented themselves triggered Pamela's memory.

The summoning of the clans. She remembered the tales told by her old Scottish nanny. *All we need are drums and bag pipes and plenty of plaid.* Imagining the men in kilts helped to banish the rest of her shyness.

Whereas before Pamela had worried about not having enough to feed everyone, now she was anxious they'd have too much. Even the kitchen and dining room tables wouldn't hold everything. "Can we set up some trestle tables outside?" she asked John.

"Good idea." He signaled for Vey to come to them. "I'll get the men started on that."

Several of the cowboys hurried over, and John gave them a string of quick instructions before heading back to her.

Pamela helped John direct people to the house and barn, answering questions about the work that needed doing as best she could. As soon as the arrivals dwindled, she headed to the house.

In the kitchen, the brick oven in the wall emitted fragrant smells of baking. Pots boiled on the stove, and the smell of roasting meat wafted from the oven. With a sense of wonder, Pamela saw dozens of jam jars stacked in a corner and hoped there'd be plenty left over.

Mr. and Mrs. Mueller, a German couple who didn't speak much English but led her to understand they were bakers, had taken over the food preparation. They beamed at her with broad smiles, while pointing out several layer cakes and pies centered on the table in the midst of more food offerings.

Mrs. Reiner, stirring something in a pot on the stove, wore an expensive blue dress under her voluminous apron. She helped with the translating, although her thick accent made her almost as difficult to understand as the Muellers. But Pamela was almost sure she said Edgar the cook had gone to kill some chickens.

The Adler daughters—two tow-headed little girls—spooned cookie batter onto a tray. Under the laden table, the Mueller toddler pounded a pot with a wooden spoon.

With a clatter of German and broken English, they shooed Pamela out of her own kitchen.

Bemused, she walked into the hallway. Hearing female voices coming from the parlor, she headed in that direction.

"That cut on Harrison's arm has taken forever to heal."

Pamela paused in the doorway. The smell of ammonia greeted her.

A woman rubbed a crumpled newspaper over the glass of a partially-opened window that allowed fresh air into the room. "I finally took out the stitches two days ago. I wish we had a doctor in this town. I couldn't handle a worse injury."

"Yes, you could, Addy," said an older woman sweeping the floor. "We have no choice but to cope with whatever happens, whether childbirth, injury, illness, or death. I've birthed five children with only my husband at my side, nursed them all when they fell ill. Set broken arms. Buried two. Helped you deliver Tyler."

A young woman, her stomach extended by pregnancy, flicked a feather duster over a marble-topped table next to the settee. "I hear they use chloroform or some such medicine to keep a woman from feeling pains during the birthing time."

"Sounds like a miracle," the woman at the window said tartly. "And as unlikely to happen in Sweetwater Springs as fleas are to fly."

The town doesn't have a physician? Appalled by what she'd just learned, Pamela swept into the room. "I couldn't help overhearing, ladies. Sweetwater Springs definitely needs a doctor!"

The one by the window just shrugged.

But the young lady stopped her dusting and placed a hand on her extended stomach. "Can you get us one, Mrs. Carter?" she asked with a begging look in her brown eyes.

"Yes," Pamela rashly promised. "But I don't know that I can work a miracle and have one here by your time...." She included the other women in her glance. "I apologize for not remembering your names. I've met so many people today."

"I'm Addy Dunn," said the window cleaner. "My husband

Harrison and I have a small ranch in Green Valley. We have one son, Tyler, who's probably out playing with the children."

The older woman had fuzzed blond-and-white curls and a bulldog chin. "I'm Mrs. Pendell. My husband and I work for the Dunns."

"And I'm Marybeth Ward," the expectant mother said. "I have three months yet to go." Her voice shook.

"I'll do my best," Pamela said. "Tomorrow, I'll write a letter to my friend in Boston, asking for her help. She can scour Boston for an available doctor. And if she can't find one willing to move here, I'll have her write letters to every medical school in the United States and Europe to find a man who's about to graduate and needs to set up a practice."

Marybeth clasped her hands together. "Oh, thank you, ma'am. Even if he's not here by my delivery time, just knowing I'd have someone to turn to if my baby became ill…" Her voice broke.

"I know," Pamela said with compassion.

"Yes, having someone who could save our babies…or at least more of our babies, would be a godsend." Mrs. Dunn straightened. "Perhaps we'll have fewer small graves in the future."

Silence followed her words. Pamela thought of John's sister Sarah, of her own future children. *Yes, please, God.*

"We certainly are grateful." Mrs. Pendell waved toward the doorway. "The three of us are setting your parlor to rights, Mrs. Carter. You're not needed here, and I'm sure you have far more important things to do than clean in here."

Pamela smiled and thanked them. She left the room, deciding to venture outdoors to see if her help was needed there.

By the horse trough with its long-handled pump, several women had set up tubs on benches under the shade of the trees and were busy at washboards, scrubbing wet clothing up and down. *Primitive.* Pamela made a mental note to inquire on the price of a modern washer. Perhaps, they could afford to acquire one.

A mountain of men's clothing lay in a pile. Two young girls who looked about Nick's age sorted through the stack, gathering up all the white garments. A load of bedding lay a few yards away. Pamela recognized the covers she'd stripped off the bed yesterday.

She peeked into a tub to see lace curtains soaking in soapy water. "Oh, my. Every scrap of material on the ranch will be clean."

"Aye," said a stout woman with a heavy Irish accent.

Pamela remembered she had a Gaelic first name that sounded something like Key-wreck.

"Once we're finished, you'll have an easier time staying on top of the laundry every week." She tsk-tsked. "I don't think those men have washed clothes since Dora died—God rest her soul. Would have taken you a week to work through this huge load."

Probably longer, since I would have had to research what to do. But using a washboard and tub looked easy enough. *Well,* Pamela amended. *A great deal of hard labor, but not so difficult to figure out how to do.*

"We'll be running out of clothesline before long." The woman didn't stop her up-and-down scrubbing of a sheet against the washboard.

Pamela glanced at the trees. "I'll have some of the men string ropes."

"Ah, a good solution, that is. I didn't want to be draping them over a dirty fence."

"I agree."

"Away with ya, now, Mrs. Carter. You just have those lines put up and leave the washing to us."

Pamela looked around for her husband, wondering what he was up to. She saw Nick unhitching a team from a wagon and hurried over to the boy. "Do you know where Mr. Carter is?"

"Last I saw him, he was in the barn."

Pamela glanced over at the huge structure. She hadn't yet been inside and chewed on her lip, thinking.

"Can I help you with something, Miz Carter?" Nick asked.

She explained what she needed for laundry lines.

He gave her a nod of understanding. "Don't you worry none. I'll see to it."

Pamela let out a deep breath. "Thank you." She turned, wondering where to head next. Movement in the fenced area by the kitchen caught her eye.

With a sense of finally treading on familiar ground, figuratively and literally, Pamela strode to the garden. On one side, several cowboys dug up the dirt, directed by a thin woman with the air of a commanding general, while nearby, a man knelt, planting seeds.

Pamela gathered up her skirt and walked between rows of young plantings brought by her guests and already tucked into the dirt. The couple's last name was Murphy, but their first names escaped her.

Mr. Murphy looked up and gave her a gentle smile and a nod. But he didn't stop his rhythmic movements, punching holes in the dirt with his forefinger and dropping in seeds.

The sharp-faced woman flicked her hand at Pamela in a shooing motion. "My husband Thomas—" Mrs. Murphy announced "—knows his way around a garden far better than any man or woman in these parts. You just leave the planting to us, Mrs. Carter."

Something about the couple's generosity brought a mist of gratitude to her eyes. "Thank you, Mrs. Murphy. And when Mr. Carter and I harvest, prepare, and serve the bounty from this garden, we'll be thanking you then, too."

The woman's sniff didn't hide the gratification in her eyes. "Thank the Almighty, as is proper, Mrs. Carter."

"I can do both, Mrs. Murphy," Pamela said gently. "There's plenty of gratitude to go around."

The woman gave a nod of acceptance and turned back toward her planting.

Pamela walked away. *Prickly woman.* She realized that if she'd met Mrs. Murphy under other circumstances, she probably would have taken a dislike to the woman. *But how can I be anything but appreciative of someone who drove a long distance to spend her day laboring in someone else's dirt?*

Not knowing where to head next, Pamela stopped in the shade of the big oak tree.

She saw her husband sanding the porch railing and paused a moment to watch him, feeling secret pride that he belonged to her.

John straightened and spotted her. He waved and shot a grin her way before bending back to his task.

Pamela did a slow turn, surveying the bustle around her. Several men painted the house, a few on each side. Others worked on replacing the porch's rotten floorboards. They'd moved the crates off the porch. Pieces of conversations drifted her way.

Many hands make light work. She'd never before realized the truth of that adage.

Pamela took a deep breath and soaked up the sense of community from this group of strangers, who by rolling up their sleeves and pitching in to help, had shown tangible care for their neighbors.

With a sense of wonder, Pamela realized she felt at home on this ranch, with these people. Somewhere in the last hours, she'd lost her sense of shyness, her discomfort with strangers. *They're no longer strangers, even if I don't know their names. And I have something to contribute to this community. They need me too.*

A group of older children dashed by, laughing and shouting, engaged in a boisterous game of tag.

Nick, walking back from the horse pasture, paused to watch. His face displayed what she guessed was longing.

She glanced at the row of vehicles and realized the boy had unhitched all the horses and turned them loose in the pasture.

Go play, Nick, she urged, sensing he stood on the edge of rejoining his friends, embracing life. She sent up a prayer, asking for an angel to give the boy a little push.

As if in response to her petition. Nick rocked forward, then plunged into the group, throwing off his cares and becoming a child again.

Pamela wanted to cheer, and she wanted to weep. Instead, she blinked away the tears and rolled up her sleeves. She'd join the cleaning crew in the house. *Goodness knows there's plenty to do there.*

But this time, the thought of the tasks didn't overwhelm her. Instead, she relished the idea of making new friends while putting her home in order. Pamela took eager steps to the half-painted house, and gladness filled her heart.

After supper and leaving the kitchen spotless, the housewives collected their empty pots, pans, and eating utensils, and bundled tired, dirty children into their wagons and buggies. The men gathered their tools. With waves and calls of "good-bye," riders and wagons began their trek home.

John slipped his arm around Pamela's waist, and she leaned into him. Around them, Nick and the other hands spread out, watching as the crowd thinned.

"Got things ship-shape." Shoah slapped the dust from his pants. "Good thing days are long, given the ride home those folks have."

"Good thing there'll be a full moon tonight," Beans echoed.

Vey took off his hat and fluffed out his matted hair. "Can't recall ever seeing so many folk in one place, no siree. Not even in those few times I set foot in Reverend Norton's church."

John laughed, glanced down at Pamela, and winked. "We got us a special attraction," he drawled.

Pamela wrinkled her nose at him. "You make me sound like a circus."

He gave her his skin-crinkling smile and jerked his head

toward the house. "Water's boiling on the stove for your…ablutions. I have some things to go over with the boys. Then we'll head over to the hot springs for our new Saturday night ritual."

Frank let out a dramatic groan. "It's only Friday!"

Everyone laughed.

John shook his head. "*I'll* be bathing, and what you smelly bunch do is your own business. I don't have to sleep in the bunkhouse."

Pamela left them, the sound of their good-natured ribbing following her.

She cast an admiring glance at the pristine white exterior, gray trim, and black door, glistening with still-wet paint. The painters had left the steps and a broad swath across the porch floor alone, so people could go in and out of the house. The windowboxes held plants that hopefully soon would bloom.

Once inside, she inhaled the air, redolent of beeswax and lemon. Not a speck of dust lay on any surface. Even the kitchen gleamed with cleanliness. Before everyone left, the Muellers had plenty of help with scouring the dishes and the room.

Pamela touched the table, smoothing a wrinkle from the blue-and-white checked tablecloth, a gift from the Addisons. With a towel, she picked up the handle of a pot of water and carried it upstairs, wishing for a bathtub with running water.

But in the bedroom, she found the tin tub already full of tepid water and realized that with a husband as solicitous of her comfort as John, she could get by without indoor plumbing.

Pamela poured in the hot water, undressed, and stepped into the tub. She took her time bathing, allowing her sore muscles to soak, and breathing in the scent of orange blossom.

She'd just dressed and gone downstairs when the plaintive sound of violin music made her heart kick up. She recognized the tune from a favorite hymn.

Pamela hurried down the hall and out the door, lured by the sound like the children of Hamelin by the Piped Piper.

The full moon bathed the yard in a milky glow.

Nick stood under an oak, the new violin tucked under his chin. He flashed her a grin, the first one she'd ever seen on him. His performance of "Simple Gifts" wasn't perfect; he hit a few scratchy notes.

But even after having attended some of the premier concerts of her day, Pamela had never heard sweeter music.

John stepped out of the shadows and walked to her, grinning as he drew close.

Pamela looked from the boy to her husband. "Whatever are you two doing?"

"I told you I had a surprise for you." John hugged her, then grinned at his godson. "I made a request of Nick, which he has been kind enough to honor. Although at first he protested that he hadn't played in months, after running off to the barn to practice a few rounds, he agreed."

John extended his hand. "May I have this dance, Mrs. Carter?"

Pamela's cheeks grew warm with pleasure. "You may, indeed, Mr. Carter."

Nick performed the song several times. Each round became smoother and more proficient.

John swung her into a turn.

In a dreamy daze, Pamela danced with her husband, remembering their first waltz. When they'd danced in Boston, she'd felt as if they were flying.

But tonight, John kept their steps languid. As they moved to the music, he held her close, looking into her eyes.

Her whole body tingled. *And when we find ourselves in the place just right... 'Twill be in the valley of love and delight.*

John slowed them until they swayed in place.

Nick stepped back, fading in the darkness until he disappeared from sight. The music was only a slight thread on the breeze, romantic and enticing.

"Compared to Boston, we have a simple life?" John made the statement a question.

"'Tis the gift to come down where we ought to be," Pamela quoted the second line of the chorus.

John pressed a kiss to her forehead. "When Nick's family died, and suddenly we had no womenfolk, I thought Dora and Marcy had taken the heart of the ranch with them to the grave. And, indeed, they had for a time. But you, dearest Pamela, have brought the heart back to us. To me."

She let out a happy sigh.

His arms tightened around her. "You, my wife, are such a delight to me. You've brought warmth and love to all of us, and I'm so very blessed. You are my beloved bride, the wife of my heart."

His words brought tears of joy to her eyes. She reached up to cup his face, feeling the stubble of his beard on her palm. "I've found my right place, John, here in your arms…in this valley."

With a scooping movement, he swept her off her feet.

The sudden action made her squeal and hold him tightly around his neck, laughing.

He gave her a lingering kiss before carrying her toward the house and over the threshold of their new life.

THE END

A Note To My Readers

Thank you so much for reading *Beneath Montana's Sky*. John and Pamela Carter's story marks the beginning of *The Montana Sky Series*, and you will see the two of them again in almost every book. Many of the characters in *Beneath Montana's Sky* will also have their own stories set in the 1890s. Elizabeth Hamilton and Nick Sanders in *Wild Montana Sky* and *Montana Sky Christmas*. Wyatt Thompson in *Starry Montana Sky*, Tyler Dunn in *Painted Montana Sky*, Joshua Norton in *Glorious Montana Sky*.

In the 1880s-set *Mail-Order Brides of the West* series, brave young ladies will travel to Montana Territory, hoping to find love and a new life in Sweetwater Springs.

Beneath Montana's Sky is also available in foreign language translations:

Spanish: Bajo el Cielo de Montana
Italian: Sotto i cieli del Montana
German: Unter Dem Himmel Von Montana (Summer 2015)

To learn about future books, sign up for Debra Holland's newsletter: http://drdebraholland.com

More Books by Debra Holland

MONTANA SKY SERIES
In chronological order:

1882
Beneath Montana's Sky

1886
Mail-Order Brides of the West: Trudy
Mail-Order Brides of the West: Lina
Mail-Order Brides of the West: Darcy
Mail-Order Brides of the West: Prudence (Summer 2015)

1890s
Wild Montana Sky
Starry Montana Sky
Stormy Montana Sky
Montana Sky Christmas: A Sweetwater Springs Short Story
Collection
A Valentine's Choice: A Montana Sky Holiday Novella
Painted Montana Sky: A Sweetwater Springs Novella
Glorious Montana Sky
Healing Montana Sky (October 2015)
Sweetwater Springs Christmas: A Montana Sky Short Story
Anthology
Sweetwater Springs Scrooge: A Montana Sky Holiday Short
Story

2015
Angel in Paradise: A Montana Sky Contemporary Short Story

About Debra Holland

New York Times and *USA Today* Bestselling author Debra Holland is a three-time Romance Writers of America Golden Heart finalist and a one-time winner. She is the author of The Montana Sky Series, sweet, historical Western romances, and The Gods' Dream Trilogy, fantasy romance. In February 2013, Amazon selected *Starry Montana Sky* as a top 50 Greatest Love Story pick.

Debra has written a nonfiction book, *The Essential Guide to Grief and Grieving* from Alpha Books (a subsidiary of Penguin). She has a free ebooklet available on her website, http://drdebraholland.com: *58 Tips for Getting What You Want From a Difficult Conversation.*

You can contact Debra and sign up for her newsletter at:
Website: http://drdebraholland.com

Also look for her:
Facebook: https://www.facebook.com/debra.holland.731
Twitter: http://twitter.com/drdebraholland
Blog: http://drdebraholland.blogspot.com

Made in the USA
Monee, IL
11 August 2024

63666475R00094